Moon Hollow

MOON HOLLOW

E.B. WHEELER

Rowan Ridge
Press

OTHER BOOKS BY E.B. WHEELER

British Historical Fiction

Born to Treason

Wishwood (Westwood Gothic)

The Royalist's Daughter

The Haunting of Springett Hall

Utah Historical Fiction

The Bone Map

No Peace with the Dawn (with Jeffery Bateman)

Home Again Blues (A Tenny Mateo Mystery)

Bootleggers & Basil (In *Pathways to the Heart*)

Letters from the Homefront

Utah Women: Pioneers, Poets & Politicians

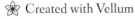

For Dan

My FAMILY CALLED ME MANY THINGS, BUT "troublesome" bothered me the most. Silly or awkward or even naughty could be endearing, but no one loved trouble.

Especially not Aunt Prudence.

If I ever had any doubts that she was right about me, I only had to compare myself to my aptly-named cousin, Walk-by-Faith Darbury. We sat close together near the window in the downstairs parlour like a painting of the sun and moon. Faith smiled dreamily as she stitched a mourning dove onto a bed curtain panel, her blonde hair in perfect ringlets, her posture straight, and the white lace on her collar and sleeves as pure as summer clouds. I had pinned my dark hair back to keep it out of my eyes, dirt from the garden clung to my skirt hem, and I held my tongue between my teeth as I worked on a difficult stitch.

My needle dawdled over an image of Aesop's fox and grapes, and though it defied the edifying moral of the fable, I had stitched the grapes low enough that the fox might snatch a few.

Aunt Prudence sailed into the parlour, her dark, tightly-laced bodice and puffed sleeves giving her the appearance of a carrion crow circling a battlefield. Faith bent her head over her neat stitches, her fingers trembling. My aunt's eyes lingered on her daughter's work. Her pinched lips worked as if she were forging some sharp words.

Before Aunt Prudence could speak, I slid my needle free and let it drop. It plinked on the stone floor.

"Oh! Watch your feet, aunt!" I made a show of fumbling after it.

"So clumsy, Jael!" Aunt Prudence stepped back as if I were contagious. "And look—how silly! You're stitching too many grapes."

"Sour grapes," I said.

Faith drew a sharp breath at my tone.

Aunt Prudence narrowed her eyes. "What?"

I raised my face, trying to imitate the liquid innocence of Faith's gaze. "The fox says they're sour, though how can he know for certain unless he tastes them?"

"You must have dandelion fluff for brains. You're wasting time and thread. Both are precious."

I threaded my needle once again and held it poised to stab the fabric. "Does Father not send enough for my upkeep, then?" She was as cautious with the care of my money as her name suggested, for I never saw a shilling of it.

My aunt flushed. "That is beside the point! You know what the scriptures tell us: 'Redeem the time because your days are evil.'"

"They certainly feel that way sometimes." I punched the needle through the fabric, starting on another grape. But what if the fox found them to be sour after all?

"Stand up," Aunt Prudence commanded.

I obeyed.

"You look a mess. Straighten your back, child. Do you want people to think I raised you to be slovenly?"

"No, madam, I'd not want them to know anything about it."

Faith stifled another noise. Possibly a giggle. I pinched my lips together so I would not smile in response.

Aunt Prudence gave my ear a tweak. "Mutton-brained brat! I hope at Moon Hollow you remember to think before you speak."

I rubbed my ear. At eighteen, I ought to be too old for ear tweaking, but Aunt Prudence had other ideas.

Moon Hollow, though. That was the home of Aunt Berenice, whom Aunt Prudence rated even more wicked than me. It might be enjoyable to change one set of drafty halls for another, but I could not imagine Aunt Prudence meant to please me. Maybe she meant to punish Aunt Berenice with a visit.

"I'm not sure why Moon Hollow would improve me," I said. "Are we going?"

"I'm sending you there."

I glanced at Faith—who had gone sickly pale—and back at my aunt, my thoughts swirling like the dandelion fluff that must indeed have floated through my head. "For... for how long?"

"That is no longer my concern. I have done my duty as well as possible with such an ungrateful, fool-headed wench, and now I wash my hands of you."

Like Lady Macbeth trying to rid herself of the spot. My throat tightened, and I swallowed a taste like rotten cider. There was nothing to say. I had outstayed my welcome once again. Aunt Prudence would pass me on as thoughtlessly as a worn-out gown. I could only curtsey—back straight as a spindle—and watch Aunt Prudence bustle out of the room.

I sat heavily. "I suppose I should have expected that," I said as much to myself as to Faith.

No one wanted to keep me around forever. I did not think I had been especially wicked lately, though, and Aunt Prudence rejoiced in both the stipend from my trust and bragging about how good she was to her poor sister's orphaned child. Not that I'm really an orphan, but when Father remarried after Mother's death, he did not want to clutter up his new household with reminders of the past. He packed me off, still wearing black for my mother, to any of her family who would tolerate me. As it was the year of our Lord 1634, that meant Aunt Prudence had done so for three years: the longest of any relative so far.

"Oh, Jael, I'm so sorry!" Faith set her needlework aside and embraced me.

"I will miss you, dearest." I clung to her, wishing I could carry some of her warmth and goodness with me. "But don't fret yourself over me."

"But 'tis my fault!"

"Oh?" I forced a teasing tone. "Did you ask your mama to send me away? Or did you teach me to be so disrespectful that she would grow tired of me?"

"Of course not! I suppose you should not speak to her in such a way, though you've always been able to make me laugh—"

"I have played a good fool for you, have I not, my dear?" I said.

Faith had been such a quiet, sad creature when another uncle—one with great, frightening eyebrows—tired of me and sent me to Aunt Prudence. But it had not been hard to make my cousin smile. At least someone in my family had found me tolerable, but now I would lose her, too. An ache rose in my chest, but I refused to acknowledge it. With each new dismissal, the pain burrowed deeper, but so did the understanding that no one cared for my tears. I never let them show.

"You're not a fool," Faith said, "but I know how often you have played my whipping boy."

I shrugged. "I cannot help being in trouble any more than you can help being good."

Faith burst into tears again. "I heard Mama talking to Papa. She is afraid you will distract Sir Godfrey from me."

I laughed, nearly letting it choke into a sob. "That's silly talk. I've seen the way Sir Godfrey looks at you. He will not be distracted."

A smile stole onto her face for a moment. "I hope it may be so... oh, but that is why Mama is sending you to that awful place!"

"Is it so awful?" I felt a glimmer of hopeful curiosity. "I suppose it must be because everyone says so, but I've never understood why. Have you ever visited?"

"Never!" Faith looked around as if fearing someone would overhear. "They say 'tis haunted."

"What respectable old place is not? Just this week, I thought I saw a white figure gliding up the stairs where the old tower used to be."

"Oh, you must be jesting! Do not say it! The white lady only appears before a disaster."

A shiver ran over my skin. I had not heard that family legend, but probably my eyes had only played tricks on me, anyway. I made myself smile. "I will certainly miss you, so I suppose that is a disaster. But Moon Hollow's ghosts cannot be much more frightening than yours."

"I wish you could be serious!" Faith squeezed my hands. "I met Aunt Berenice once. She had such a horrid face. And Mother has hinted that her husband is not at all honest."

"I suppose with a name like Barabbas, he could not be. Do you suppose his parents actually read the Bible or just opened it and stuck their finger on a name?"

I wondered the same about my parents. Did they think naming a child after a woman who slew kings with tent stakes would make her grow up to be good? Better to have Puritan parents who burdened their children with holy mouthfuls such as Walk-by-Faith and Grant-me-Strength.

Faith's chuckle gurgled through her tears. "Oh, Jael, you *are* wicked. What am I going to do without you to make me laugh?"

"You will soon have Sir Godfrey to keep you happy."

I did not doubt Faith's happiness. And perhaps I was only reaping what I sowed, being banished to Moon Hollow. Maybe, if it was such a wicked place, I would feel at home there. But that was a dangerous thought. I could not allow myself to hope for anything, going begging as I did from relative to relative. That did not mean, though, that this change had to be a disaster.

After a tense supper that evening, I made my way alone to my chamber. The candles flickered low in their sconces, throwing dancing shadows across the cold, stone corridor. I shivered and walked faster.

In the corner of my eye, I once again caught a glimpse of a white shape drifting toward the stairs to the tower. The tower that had collapsed with a poor lady inside it.

I refused to look closer but hurried to my room and bolted the door behind me.

2

THE DAY I WAS TO LEAVE THE DARBURYS, I AWOKE IN THE gray predawn light. A heavy feeling sat in my stomach like a lump of uncooked bread dough. I dressed as neatly as I could, struggling to tighten my laces alone, and tiptoed down the silent corridor to the great hall.

My trunks waited by the front doors, lonely stumbling blocks in the gloom. I strolled a circuit of the great hall, taking in the tapestries and family portraits that had surrounded me for the last three years. These impassive ancestors were the only ones who would see me off. Faith had wanted to say goodbye one more time, but I would not wake her. She would forget me as easily as the rest of the family now that she had Sir Godfrey. This way, we would all have a fresh start. I took a deep breath, but it did nothing to ease the tightness in my stomach.

The horse-groom popped his head in the door, holding a lantern that sent long shadows reaching for me. "Ready, Mistress?"

I hesitated, looking back toward the chamber where Faith

slept. Then I nodded and turned my back on my erstwhile home to march into the dewy chill. The pale edge of the moon slipped below the western horizon, and the cold seeped into my skin. I climbed into the carriage as the coachman secured my trunks, and then we creaked away over the bumpy road.

Fields and woods rolled by, but I hardly registered them, imagining Moon Hollow. Was it possible to escape who I had been with this new start? Aunt Prudence did not like Aunt Berenice, so maybe she would not have poisoned her mind by telling her what I was. *Troublesome. Slovenly wench. Fool-headed girl.* But Faith's warning came back to me: The white lady portended disaster.

We passed several hamlets of snug stone cottages with thatched roofs, stopping only once to refresh ourselves at an inn.

As the day waned toward evening, the carriage slowed again. I perked up and studied the little village made up of craftsmen's shops, farmers' homes, and a tidy church that had survived the iconoclasts of the Reformation. A few women gossiping at the community well paused to return my curious stare.

A man on horseback galloped down the dusty village lane toward us. The women shouted and shook ruddy fists, and my coachman swore, but the rider rushed past. I leaned out the window, but he had already vanished around a wooded bend.

Another horseman rode hard behind him. His chestnut horse swept by, and I caught a glimpse of the rider's determined profile. This time, the village gossips did not scold, but kept their eyes downcast and returned to their business.

I pursed my lips and drew my head back in. Horse races through the village square? Maniacs. At least I would not be the only wicked person in the neighborhood, though. I settled back into my seat, tapping my fingers and watching for Moon Hollow.

Hoofbeats approached from behind the carriage.

"Halt!" a stern male voice called.

I looked out the curtain to find the rider on the chestnut gelding trotting alongside the carriage. My coachman reined in, and the rider's attention focused on me. He wore his sandy brown hair fashionably long, and his sharp face was more interesting than handsome, reminding me of the fox from my needlework.

My horse-groom sputtered a protest at being stopped. The rider dismissed him with a glance and rested his hand on a pistol sheathed at the front of his saddle.

"What is the meaning of this?" I wondered for a moment if the rider might be a highwayman, but he wore no mask, and his satin doublet and polished black leather boots were unfit for rough living.

"I was chasing a suspected bandit." He looked past me into the carriage, where the small trunk with my few valuables sat beside me, and he smirked as if life were a joke that he did not find very clever.

I leaned to block his view. "And you think your robber transformed from horse and rider to carriage, horse, lady, and two manservants?"

His smirk turned to a grin. "For such a pretty songbird, you sing a mocking tune. You might be confederate with the villain."

"Is he the villain? *He* only rode too fast. *You* have stopped my carriage."

"You are right to question my word." The bitterness returned to his expression. "But I would be a bold highwayman to rob a carriage in the middle of a village."

"And yet, I think the villagers fear you."

His gaze cut back to me. "Perhaps you are not a songbird, then, but a keen-eyed falcon."

My cheeks warmed. "I am not any sort of a bird. I am Mistress Jael Hawkins, going to visit my aunt Berenice Coffin at Moon Hollow."

Some of the amusement drained from his face, and he studied me. "To Moon Hollow? I imagine you are not staying long."

"I know not how long. Perhaps for the rest of my life."

"That, I hope, will not be the case!"

I could not decide if he was joking. "And who are you to speak so rudely to a strange lady?"

"Sebastian Westwood, my lady. And have no fear. I speak rudely to everyone. Keep your keen eyes open at Moon Hollow, though. You'll have need to be watchful."

He touched his hat and rode off, leaving me with a sense of foreboding.

The carriage rumbled on, turning onto a shaded lane. It dipped down into a carefully groomed park with wide expanses of turf and groves of trees. But there was no movement. The landscape seemed strangely desolate despite the green.

And the house. It had a stark, symmetrical front, with two towers framing an entryway and two wings stretching away from the center. The right-hand side of the house looked newer, the stones less worn, constructed more recently to bring the house into fashion. Dozens of gray windows stared out onto the empty turf like the glassy eyes of a corpse. I shuddered and looked away.

The carriage rolled to a stop. The horse-groom helped me down, and before I had time to ask any questions, he unloaded my trunks and hopped back up next to the coachman. The carriage turned away, leaving me on my own in front of Moon Hollow.

I approached the front door and grasped the brass ring to knock. It was cold against my palm, and I let it drop with a heavy clang.

After a few minutes, the door crept open. A young man peeked his head around, then swung the door open, scanning the landscape as though expecting an ambush. Finally, his gaze fell on me. When he straightened, he looked more like a proper porter: a tall, almost gawky young man with short-cropped red hair and a somber black doublet that highlighted his pale skin.

"Good morrow," I said, craning my neck to meet his eyes. "I am Jael Hawkins. I've come to see my Aunt, Mistress Coffin."

He glanced over his shoulder and licked his lips nervously. "J-just a moment. I will fetch m-my mistress."

The porter allowed me into the front hall and hauled my trunk inside before going in search of my aunt.

A polished wood staircase wrapped around both sides of the room like two eels meeting on the landing above. The bottom of the walls was paneled in golden oak, and Biblical characters painted directly on the white plaster marched around the upper part of the room. Another Puritan branch of the family, I wagered. Beeswax candles filled the front hall with their light and sweet scent, but not much sunlight penetrated the room from the single, tall window. Most of the windows I'd seen outside were false, giving only the illusion of symmetry and expensive glass.

"What is this, then?"

I whirled to see a lumpy sort of man striding toward me. He had a paunchy stomach, a round face, and bulging eyes that narrowed when he took in my dusty dress and the trunk behind me.

"What business do you have here?" He glared at me like I was a dog begging for scraps.

I lifted my chin, but inwardly I shrank from his disdain. Not a promising start.

"Hinton?" a man's voice called. "Do we have another guest?"

The lumpy man assumed a deferential expression and bowed as a large man dressed in dark satin and velvet entered the great hall. No doubt this was my Uncle Barabbas. I curtseyed deeply and rose to find his eyes on me. He was quickly joined by a lady and a girl about twelve, also finely dressed. The lady—my aunt, I guessed—was also a bit stout with a handsome face. Strange. Faith had said Aunt Berenice looked horrid. I found a likeness to Aunt Prudence in her tight lips and military bearing, though. My chest tightened at the unpleasant familiarity.

The girl—a cousin of mine?— was as thin as a stalk of barley and kept her pale face downcast, stealing occasional glances at me with large gray eyes. She held a little spaniel close and scratched its ears. Her sad, shy expression reminded me of Faith, and my heart went out to her.

The lumpy man called Hinton swept me a dismissive glance and said, "Master Coffin, this person just arrived. It appears she has brought baggage."

All eyes turned to me.

"I am Jael," I said. This did not seem to abate anyone's confusion. I appealed to my aunt. "Your niece, Jael Hawkins. Certainly, Aunt Prudence wrote that I was coming?"

"She did." Aunt Berenice said. "I had not written her back yet about the best time…"

The room descended into stifling silence. I clenched my hands. Was I to be sent away without even having moved in?

And where would I go? Did I have an aunt or cousin twice removed or some such relation who had not yet rejected me?

"So, Prudence sent you here anyway." Aunt Berenice glared out through the one window. "A nasty trick from my sister, but it sounds like her."

There was no way to answer that that would not make me seem an ungrateful wretch, so I kept my naughty mouth shut.

"We always have a place for family," Aunt Berenice said, stepping forward. The keys on her belt jangled beside a twisted sort of root or carved branch she kept tied there. "There are so many people in and out, it might be a little chaotic, but I'm sure you'll forgive us."

My breathing eased a little. "There is nothing to forgive. I look forward to knowing you. I can keep my cousin company."

The girl glanced up at me, her gray eyes even wider. In surprise, or fear?

"Don't mind Sybil," Uncle said. "She's easily upset. Moll?"

A young woman came forward. Her skin was dark and a white coif covered her ebony hair. A Moor? I tried not to stare. She wore a lace collar too fine for a servant, but her sleeves bore no slashing or beadwork like the family or a fine guest might show off. In fact, she was dressed rather like me, though her clothes were newer.

Moll cast me a suspicious glance and then took Sybil gently by the arm and guided her away.

Aunt waited for them to exit the hall, then said, "I imagine my sister sent you here because she failed to find you a husband in her little corner of the world. Surprising. You're comely enough and come from a good family."

"I... I don't think she tried very hard," I said. "In fact, I don't think she tried at all."

"Of course!" Aunt Berenice's eyes brightened with understanding. "She was busy getting rid of those girls of hers. The ones with the ridiculous names. Pray-for-Deliverance. Grant-me-Virtue."

I fought to keep a laugh from my voice. "Cousin Grant is male, my lady. Though, he is married, too."

Aunt Berenice snorted. "Well, now my sister is getting you out of the way of that last plain-looking daughter of hers."

"Faith is quite pretty," I said.

"Bah! Only if she has changed greatly since I last saw her. Well, I doubt her features are as fine as yours." Aunt Berenice looked to Uncle Barabbas. "You must find our niece someone to marry. It should not be difficult."

He nodded. "I agree. I'll turn something up." He said it with such confidence as if he might just stumble across a husband for me discarded beside the road.

"If only everyone knew how easy it was to pick up a husband, they would worry less for their daughters," I blurted out. Fool-headed girl. I sounded disrespectful. Why could I not keep my mouth shut?

Aunt Berenice gave me an odd look, but Uncle Barabbas laughed.

"You are right," he said. "People ought to worry less."

I dared to smile back at him. Aunt Berenice came forward and put an arm around me. I flinched before I realized she was not about to give me a shake or tweak my ear.

"You must be exhausted, poor child," Aunt Berenice said. "Robin will show you to a room," She motioned for the lanky porter. "The red room, I think."

The young man hefted my trunks and headed for the stairs with a quick, nervous gait. I scurried to follow.

"Welcome to Moon Hollow, niece," my uncle said.

His words poured warmth through me. I could not

remember another relative who had so much as spoken the word 'welcome.' Yet when I looked back to thank him, he was already in conversation with Hinton.

Just as well. Hopefully, he would forget the husband he was supposed to find for me as quickly. I had never considered marriage before, as I did not know anyone who wanted me, and I certainly did not wish to be pushed off on someone else who would see me as a burden. At least Berenice and Barabbas Coffin seemed willing to tolerate me for the time being.

Robin guided me up one side of the staircase. I glanced over to the other wing and caught Cousin Sybil watching from the shadows. I had only a moment to meet her stare, but I thought I saw a warning in her frightened gray eyes. Then Moll put an arm around her shoulder and led her away.

3

MY QUARTERS WERE IN THE OLDER SIDE OF THE HOUSE, BUT they included a withdrawing chamber as well as a bed-chamber. So much space I hardly knew what to do with it. Robin deposited my trunks in the withdrawing chamber with a thud. He looked at me curiously, as though he might ask something, but only swallowed a couple of times, his Adam's apple bobbing frantically, and hurried out.

Strange young man. Most households chose a porter who would make a striking first impression on their guests, and while Robin's height and shocking red hair were striking, he was the twitchiest manservant I'd ever met.

Finally alone, I twirled around the chambers, admiring the soft cushions on the chairs and the mattress stuffed with feathers instead of straw. Furnishings fit for an honored guest. Not a drafty room stuffed with worn out, unwanted furniture.

A knock sounded on the door.

"Enter!" I called.

Moll, the Moorish woman, walked in. She offered a shallow curtsey, her suspicious gaze never leaving me.

"Mistress Coffin asked me to check if you were settled in," she said. "The maids are busy with other guests, and I suppose you need help with your dress."

I did not miss the hint that Moll was no maid. A companion to Cousin Sybil, perhaps. If she were one of the guests, she would not have been sent to check on me. Like me, she occupied one of the odd nooks of society. We all had to know our place and stay in it, but that did not mean we truly belonged.

"I would not mind help." I had become used to fastening my bodice and stomacher myself each day and arranging my hair, but perhaps this was a chance to make a friend.

As Moll worked on my lacings, I noticed a whelk shell on a cord around her neck. She caught me staring at it and tucked it into her bodice. Her expression did not invite heart-to-heart conversation, but I have never excelled at minding my tongue.

"I have heard Moon Hollow has a ghost," I said lightly.

Moll tugged the sleeve off my arm. "Every place has its... history." She looked me in the face, her eyes hard. "There's enough trouble in the present without borrowing from the past."

She held out my robe, wrinkling her nose a little at the threadbare wool handed down from one of the cousins with the ridiculous names.

I quickly drew it on, covering my much-mended shift. "Thank you."

Moll curtseyed again and left, closing the door behind her with a snap.

I pulled the robe snuggly around me and brushed my hair, working savagely on the tangles. My eyes stung, but I squeezed them shut. Of course, I could not expect everyone to welcome me to Moon Hollow. Why should I care what anyone else in the household thought of me? My aunt and uncle had been more kind than I deserved.

Despite reassuring myself with these thoughts, I had trouble falling asleep. The red of the curtains turned hot and oppressive in the darkness, blocking out the faint moonlight from the window.

As I stared at the canopy and traced the lines of stitches with my eyes, a cry echoed through my chamber: a horrified wail.

I sat up, my heartbeat pulsing in my ears. The night was still, and no wind had ever blown with such a sound, like a soul lost and frightened. Perhaps it was a nightbird whose call I did not know.

I parted the bed curtains, and the chill of the stone room encircled me. Moonbeams spilled in through the window, lighting my room like the dawn. I eased out of the bed, searching for slippers.

The sound came again, rolling down the corridor and growing to end in a high, very human scream.

Had some disaster befallen Moon Hollow? Did I carry ill-fortune like fleas on a dog? That man, Sebastian Westwood, had mentioned bandits. Perhaps burglars had broken in and were murdering the household. I put my hand on the door.

But if I went out, I would only be in the way of anyone trying to defend the house.

I pressed my ear to the wood. All was silent in the corridor.

I eased the door open and peeked out, expecting to meet a scene of bloodshed. Only darkness greeted me. Except, I thought I heard very faintly the sound of weeping. I tiptoed out to find the source of the heartbreak, but the sounds stopped. All seemed peaceful in the house. Almost unnaturally quiet. With goose pimples standing all over my skin, I snuck back into my room and bolted the door.

If this was the ghost of Moon Hollow, then Faith was right: it was more frightening than her white lady.

I made my way to the window, which looked over a wide expanse of turf behind the house, leading down to a river shimmering in the moonlight. A lone figure wandered along the riverbank. Shivers ran down my spine, and I ducked out of sight. If I were not so aware of the chill and the pounding of my pulse, I would think it was a nightmare.

When I looked again, the figure was gone. The house had grown perfectly still, and I heard nothing but, perhaps, a faint rustling in the corridor. This time, I did not dare to look out.

"TIME FOR PRAYERS!"

I started awake. "What?" Was I back under Aunt Prudence's thumb?

The bed curtains jerked open, and Moll stared down at me. "Master Coffin—er, your uncle—gathers all the household for prayers in the morning."

"Of course!"

I longed to keep sleeping, but then they would know I was wicked. I rolled out of bed and let Moll help me into a dress—another relic from a cousin. Not only was it out of fashion, but my work on remaking it to fit me was less than perfect. I caught Moll frowning at it. The only jewelry I could add was a string of fake pearls cast off by Aunt Prudence. It was the best I could do, but I was afraid it would not be good enough for Moon Hollow.

Moll led me down the long corridor, past the stairs and grand entrance hall, to the other wing of the house.

A boy with a bit of hay stuck in his unkempt hair raced up the stairs, nearly crashing into us from behind.

"Oi!" he said. "Mistress Moll! Mistress, uh... " he eyed me and shrugged. "M'lady. Am I late?"

Moll smiled with a kindness I had doubted she was capable of. "Just in time, Jim."

She tolerated dusty little boys, then, but not cast-off cousins.

"Whew!" Jim grinned and scurried past us.

We followed him into Uncle Barabbas's withdrawing room. Jim faced off with my uncle's lumpy, round-faced gentleman, Hinton.

"Mistress Moll said I was *not* late," Jim said.

Hinton's nostrils flared, and he plucked the bit of hay out of Jim's hair. "You must apply yourself if you want to secure your place at Moon Hollow."

He glanced at me when he said it. I pressed my lips together. I *would* apply myself.

My uncle sat at the head of the table before Aunt Berenice, Cousin Sybil, and a few well-dressed guests. Several maids and the tall porter Robin stood around the edges of the room with heads bowed. Hinton glared everyone into reverence, his bugged eyes missing nothing.

Moll sat beside Sybil, whose gray eyes remained on the little spaniel in her lap. Moll patted my cousin's hand, and Sybil looked at her with the trust a child shows a parent. Aunt Berenice motioned me to sit by her. I tried not to show my giddy relief at being acknowledged and included.

One of the guests, a handsome young man with curly, dark brown hair, gawked at me across the table before resuming a prayerful attitude.

Uncle Barabbas opened the Bible, and I braced myself for the lecture.

"Ho, everyone that thirsteth, come ye to the waters, and he that hath no money, come ye, buy and eat!"

I forgot my modest pose and looked up at Uncle Barabbas.

He winked at me and continued. "Eat ye that which is good, and let your soul delight itself in fatness." My uncle looked up at the assembled household. He patted his belly. "Sounds like good advice for the day, eh?"

A few of the guests snickered. Aunt Berenice smiled as though it were a joke she'd heard too often. Uncle set the Bible aside and offered a short prayer, then everyone scrambled back about their business. I looked around, not sure what was expected of me.

"Good morrow, Jael!" Uncle boomed. "Did you sleep well?"

"The bed is very soft." The ghosts were very loud, but I did not want to complain. They did not appear to have bothered anyone else.

"Nothing but the best at Moon Hollow! Join us in breaking your fast."

A maid placed cold meats and ale on the table. I listened while Uncle chatted with the guests about a new horse he was considering buying. He glanced at me again, and a frown creased his forehead.

"Hinton!" Uncle said. "Have the tailor—what is his name?—come to visit. I want my niece to have a new dress."

"Aye, my lord," Hinton said, his gaze brushing me with a cold appraisal.

My cheeks burned as everyone stared at me.

"Thank you, Uncle," I said tightly. I did want a new dress, but with less attention drawn to my old one. Still, I had to be grateful.

When Uncle had eaten his fill, he stood, and the meal was over.

Aunt Berenice drew me aside. "Don't mind your uncle's wagging tongue. He does not always think before he speaks." Before I could stutter out a thanks, she sighed wearily and said, "Sybil, dear, let me help you with your knitting."

And I was alone again. I took a deep breath. Thus far, my Coffin family did not despise or dislike me. They even seemed inclined to be kind in their way. How long until I ruined that?

The servants began their daily chores of cleaning and mending. They paid me little heed as I strolled through the corridors and parlors, except Hinton, whose bug-eyed stare discouraged me from venturing near the servants' realm. None of the maids looked tired or nervous as I suspected they would if they had heard the screams in the night. If I was going to satisfy my curiosity, I needed to go outside and see for myself.

I found a door leading out to the gardens and river behind the house. The cool, damp scent of grass and water welcomed me. A peacock ruffled his long feathers and strutted away, uttering his plaintive call.

The cry almost sounded like the wail I had heard. The eyes on the peacock's feathers shimmered in the morning light. Did peacocks call at night? I did not think so. And as piercing as their cry might be, it was not the same as the human scream I had heard.

The river murmured dark and deep along its way, and the grass grew thick along its edge. Yet the grass was trampled flat in one spot. I thought I could make out bootprints leading into the water.

"Good morrow, mistress!"

I looked up to find the boy who'd had the bit of hay in his hair—Jim—grinning at me.

"Good morrow," I said. "I take it you live here at Moon Hollow?"

"I'm the stableboy. My Pa says if I work hard, I might be a horse-groom someday."

"I'm sure your Pa is correct. Do you like horses?"

"Course I do! Don't you?"

"I certainly appreciate them. I suppose I would have to get to know them better to see if I liked them."

He gave me an appraising look and puffed out his chest. "I think I could let you meet them. How long are you staying at Moon Hollow?"

"I... I'm not sure."

He did not seem to find this unusual. "Need to warn you, then. Don't get too near the river. 'Tis all sorts of dangerous."

"Is it?"

"Jim!" a male voice called. "What have I told you?"

The handsome guest with the dark hair strolled toward us.

Jim flushed, turning the tips of his ears pink. "You said that I ought not to chatter on or be such a saucebox, sir."

"Exactly right. Back to work with you." The young man's tone was authoritative but not unkind. As Jim ran off, the dark-haired man smiled at me. "Are you lost, Mistress..."

"Jael Hawkins. But I'm not lost, just exploring."

"I'm Jonas Grubb, the schoolmaster. I lease the lodge over yonder from your aunt and uncle. Perhaps I can show you around the estate? I don't have any students this morning, and the river can be more dangerous than it looks."

"Oh?" I asked. "That was just what young Jim was telling me."

"He talks too much, but he's an honest lad. The current runs swiftly when you get far into the river. Sometimes I have to rescue the local boys who think they can swim in it."

"Oh! How dreadful. Perhaps you should teach them to swim."

He laughed. "Then I'd never get them out of the water, and a teacher must keep his students in the classroom. There are other places where you can safely wander, though."

"No worries about bandits?" I asked.

"I've heard of local troubles with housebreakers, but they're not likely to harass you at Moon Hollow. Especially not in the daylight."

He offered his arm. I took it, but not without glancing back at the river.

"Do you ever see or hear anything strange near the river at night?" I asked.

"Ah, has someone been telling you the local ghost stories?"

"I knew there had to be a ghost!"

"That does not frighten you?" He looked a little disapproving.

"I've always thought that a ghost that belongs to a particular place seems more melancholy than dangerous."

"I wish that were the case with our ghost. Some say it lures people into the water to drown them."

"Terrible!" I shuddered. "Tell me more!"

"More?" He looked down at me. I had crossed the line and horrified the good schoolmaster. "That's not a story for young ladies."

"Nonsense!" I snapped. Master Grubb's eyes widened, and naughty girl that I am, an excuse came to me quickly. "The ghost story must be nonsense. After the first few victims, people would know better than to follow the spirit into the river."

He smiled stiffly. "Best to just stay away. See, this path over here is a lovely one."

Master Grubb led me to the gardens, and I did not look back again, but I could only think about the track leading down to the river. Had the ghost led some poor soul into the water and dragged him under? Because no ghost would leave prints, no matter how soft the mud.

❧ 4 ❧

THAT NIGHT, MOON HOLLOW HAD A NEW SET OF GUESTS AT supper—leading men from a nearby village, I gathered. Uncle Barabbas regaled us all with descriptions of the "poor ugly nag" his neighbor tried to sell him.

"I felt so bad for the beast, I almost bought it anyway!"

"Oh, husband..." Aunt Berenice rubbed her temples.

"Well, I did not, woman, so stop fretting. But 'tis a good policy to do a good turn now and then."

Aunt Berenice rolled her eyes. "Aye, my lord, but you do a good turn every other day. 'Tis expensive to be so generous."

Uncle pounded the table and laughed. "That is right! No man would dare call me cheap!"

A few of the guests chuckled and raised their glasses at that. The wine and jokes flowed freely. Aunt Berenice's smile turned strained, Moll frowned at her plate, and Sybil absent-mindedly played with her spaniel's ears. I kept my expression polite, but I watched the other guests closely. Uncle Barabbas *was* generous. Easy to take advantage of. If my aunt and uncle welcomed a wicked girl like me, what vipers might they invite into their bosom?

By the time I returned to my chambers, the moon was high and my eyes were heavy. I listened for ghostly wails, but the household settled down for sleep. Before I could do the same, though, memories of moonlit figures and footprints in the mud flitted through my mind, and I snuck over to peer out the window.

Nothing stirred but the glittery reflection of the moon in the river. I watched the hypnotic shimmer, resting my cheek on the cool stone arch of the window and letting the stillness seep into me.

A shadow moved below. I straightened, not sure what I had seen. It moved again, slinking from tree to tree, briefly visible when it crossed a stretch of turf. Did ghosts sneak through the darkness? I doubted it. But housebreakers did.

The figure paused and stared up at the house. I had the sense, for a moment, that it was looking directly at me. Then it vanished into the shrubbery.

Tempted as I was to sneak out and confront the villain, even I was not fluff-headed enough to do so. Instead, I hurried back into the corridor.

Moon Hollow crawled with people during the day, but now my footsteps echoed in the silence. I ventured to the other wing of the house, but my uncle's withdrawing chamber door was bolted shut for the night. If he could sleep through a wailing ghost, he could sleep through my shouting. Should I seek out one of the guests or servants? Whom could I trust? I turned back for my room.

Hinton stood in my path.

I yelped. The faint light of a shuttered candle lantern cast a pale yellow over one side of his face, leaving the other in shadow except for his bulging eyes. He sneered, twisting his shaded features.

"What are you doing wandering about?" he demanded.

"I could ask you the same thing!"

"It is my job to see that the household is secure. Everything must be in its place. Including you."

"Then you should be watching the grounds. I was coming to raise the hue and cry. Someone is sneaking around the river."

He squinted at me. "I will see to it. Lock yourself in your chamber."

I wanted to argue at his imperious tone, but he had the right of it. I marched back to my chambers and slammed the bolt into place. I saw no movement outside the window, but Hinton was as sneaky as a cat, appearing out of nowhere. With nothing more to do, I finally fell into a fidgety sleep.

THE NEXT MORNING, after prayer and breakfast, I caught Uncle Barabbas alone.

"Uncle, I saw something strange out my window last night."

"Oh, aye? We're said to have a ghost on our river."

"I have heard, but this looked like a person sneaking through the woods."

He laughed. "No doubt some of the local peasantry poaching fish from the river. There are not many places outside of Moon Hollow where the water is easy to reach. I pay the poachers no attention, and neither should you."

He patted my shoulder and strolled off.

Perhaps I had overreacted and let my imagination carry me away. But the shadow in the gardens had carried no poles or nets for fishing, and the figure I had seen the first night wandered the riverbank as no fisherman would. Uncle Barabbas was too kind-hearted and carefree to be suspicious, but the thought that some bandit or criminal might take advantage of my family plagued me. I knew trouble well enough to sense when it was afoot.

I fetched my boots and set off for the river. Footsteps were not easy to find in the turf, but on the muddy ground near the river, I found the marks of boots pacing back and forth. Someone searching or waiting for something. They moved downriver. I traced them until the trees and brush crowded along the bank to block my way.

I broke off a branch and tossed it out into the current. The water caught it and whisked it away, the top twigs bobbing wildly like a hand imploring help. Master Grubb was right: the river flowed fast and deep here.

The intruder must have cut through the woods, and I would have to do the same. An ideal place for bandits to hide. I glanced back toward the house. Well, no one had ever accused me of being wise.

I threaded my way through coppiced trees and brambles until the trees thinned out into an opening. The ground was cleared for crops, and in the distance, the towers of some ancient keep rose to watch over them. I skirted around fields of peas and wheat. A cluster of farmers' cottages sat near the river. Could the nighttime stalker have come from this place?

As I approached, I spotted a group of cottagers gathered outside, watching something in the center of the little hamlet.

I crept up behind one of the cottages to spy on them. Sebastian Westwood stood in their midst. He claimed to be hunting bandits, but what if he were in league with them?

His sharp face wore an expression of mild annoyance as he listened to two farmers argue.

"Jones stole my pig!"

"It was my pig, seeing as how you never paid the full price for it. I just took it back."

"I have witnesses to say I did pay full price!"

"And I have witnesses to say you did not!"

"Enough!" Sebastian raised a hand, and the two men fell silent. "You both agree that at least some payment was made for the pigs?"

"Aye, sir," Jones said carefully.

Sebastian nodded. "Butcher the pig. Divide it in half, and you each get your portion."

They stared at him in stunned silence for a few moments, both red-faced with repressed protests, then bowed and hurried away. The other onlookers dispersed as well, as if afraid he would start chopping other things in two.

Sebastian stood alone in front of the cottages, green fields stretching before him. His forehead wrinkled as he surveyed his domain, but his face slowly relaxed and his lips slowly turned up in a self-satisfied smile.

The cottagers had probably never imagined themselves governed by such a rogue. I covered my mouth, but a laugh escaped me.

Sebastian's eyes narrowed, and he scanned the quiet hamlet. I thought it better to let myself be discovered than try to run from him, so I stepped into view.

"Solomon is not appreciated in his own day," I said.

His gaze found me, and his lips twitched. "Such is the way with genius."

"You know," I said, "Solomon did not actually cut the baby in half."

Now he did smile. "I hope neither of the mothers was planning to eat it, anyway."

I laughed again. "So do I!"

"And what brings Mistress Jael, the slayer of tyrants, to Aubrey Hall? You're not here for me, I hope?"

He said it like he suspected that I had come to find him. If he had something to hide, I did not want him suspicious.

"Certainly not!" I said lightly. "I was walking along the river, as nearly as I could. I thought I was still on my uncle's estate."

"I'm afraid you've been led astray. The river will do that, you know."

"I've heard it is haunted."

"Naturally. Every brook and glade in the kingdom has its tale of unquiet spirits."

"Do you know the story?" I asked.

"I'm not a native of these parts, but I've heard bits of it."

"I suppose 'tis unfit for a lady's ears?"

"Nonsense. I will tell you the story while I accompany you home."

I was intrigued but did not want to seem too eager. "I can return on my own."

"No doubt. But, while I do not put much store in hauntings, there are still criminals at large."

I glanced back at the woods, which suddenly seemed more tangled and dark. "Very well. But only to hear the story."

He fell into step beside me. "'Tis a lady who they say haunts the river. She was once the mistress of Moon Hollow, beautiful and faithful, but her husband was a suspicious brute and believed rumors of her infidelity spread by a jealous neighbor. The husband chased her out of the house, and she fled to the river and drowned in the swift waters. Now, she lures those guilty of telling falsehoods to share her fate."

"But, that could be anyone!"

"I suppose that's the terror of it: anyone who walks near the river must assess their own honesty and may find it lacking."

"Do you walk by the river, then?" I teased.

He raised an eyebrow. "As I said, I do not believe in ghosts."

"I think I've seen one. Or I've heard one, at least."

"Interesting. What else has the keen falcon observed at Moon Hollow?"

"If you're so curious, you should look for yourself."

He smiled wickedly. "Perhaps I shall, sweet bird."

I flushed at his familiar tone, all the more embarrassed because I had invited it by being too casual with him. Yet, it had felt natural. Comfortable. "I believe you are a meddler."

"You are correct. I have an obligation."

"To Aubrey Hall, perhaps. Not to Moon Hollow."

He smiled humorlessly. "To myself. Aubrey Hall is my purgatory, and I have many sins to atone for."

With that odd comment, he left me standing on the edge of the woods at Moon Hollow.

I walked up to the house and found Hinton watching me with those suspicious, bulging eyes.

"Was that Sebastian Westwood?" he asked.

"It was."

"Your aunt and uncle would not like you associating with him."

"Believe me, I hope to do so as little as possible."

I swept into the house, but I suspected I was not finished with Master Westwood.

5

NEVERENDING CORRIDORS STRETCHED BEFORE ME IN MY dreams. The white lady drifted ahead, and I chased her, but she glided just out of reach. Sometimes my fingertips brushed the wisps of pale gauze trailing behind her, but they passed through. Tangles of cobwebs clung to my skirts and my hair. I could not brush them off. I kept running.

A shriek brought me out of my nightmare.

I sat up, my heart pounding in the quiet. The gray sky warned me it was nearly dawn.

Another scream reached me, as from somewhere far away. But it was not just the echo of my dream. I swung my feet out from the warm safety of the blankets and tiptoed to the withdrawing chamber. The corridor was quiet, and when I eased the door open, a chilly quiet met me.

I drew back to the window facing the river. Someone moved through the garden. Goose bumps raced over my skin. This was no ghost. It limped and looked behind as though being pursued. In the dim light, it reminded me of Jim, the stableboy.

His scream for help reached me through the glass.

I grabbed my robe and hurried downstairs to the garden door.

The dusky light of dawn glowed gray over a cold turf. The limping figure had vanished, but I knew what direction he had gone. Toward Sebastian's Aubrey Hall.

The woods formed a bleak gray barrier. I glanced back at Moon Hollow. It would take time to rouse the house and get help, and Jim was in danger now. I jogged to the edge of the trees and searched the ground. The path I had found before was the only way through. I braved the reaching, clawing branches of the trees to follow.

The coming dawn did not pierce the canopy of the trees, so I stumbled through the gloom, feeling as if I had slipped back into my nightmare of endless dim corridors.

A form appeared on the trail. Jim. He lay sprawled face-down in the leaves. I rushed to his side and knelt.

"Jim?"

I touched his shoulder, afraid to move him if he was injured. He still breathed, but only groaned faintly at my touch. His eyes were closed and blood oozed from his forehead.

I tore a strip from my robe and pressed it to the bleeding. Jim needed help, and I was not strong enough to move him far.

"What happened?" I asked him. "Who did this to you?"

"The river," he muttered, his eyes never opening.

His clothes were dry except. Perhaps he was delirious.

"I will get help," I told him.

I stood and scanned the woods. I was between Moon Hollow and Aubrey Hall. Jim worked at Moon Hollow. But the lad had been dragging himself away from my uncle's house toward the cottages at Aubrey Hall. Maybe the father he mentioned lived there. And farmers would already be awake at this time, ready to help.

I raced down the path, reaching the hamlet of cottages out of breath. Smoke curled up from the holes in the center of the roofs, and a few early-rising boys had already headed out the fields to shoo birds away from the crops.

"Help!" I called.

The shout brought curious farmers and their wives and children from the cottages.

"Young Jim is hurt in the woods!" I pointed.

"Send for help from the big house," one of the farmers said, and a young boy raced toward the old stone keep. The man eyed me uncertainly. "Show us where you found him."

I must have presented quite a sight, but the small crowd of men and women followed me into the woods. I reached the spot where I had left Jim.

He was gone.

"He could not have moved far," I said, as much to myself as to the others.

The skeptical expressions multiplied, but the cottagers helped me search the brush.

"What is all this trouble?" called a demanding voice.

I spun to find Sebastian striding toward us. He would believe me.

"The stableboy, Jim, was injured, here in the woods," I told him, half-jogging to keep up with his long steps as he walked past the cottagers. "Now, he's gone. He was too badly injured to move on his own. I'm sure of it."

Sebastian's forehead wrinkled. "And how did you know of this?"

I could see from their faces that it was what the cottagers

wanted to ask, too, but dared not. I prayed that the chill air would keep me from flushing.

"I heard shouting outside my window at Moon Hollow and saw him. I ran out to... to see what was happening."

"And you came to Aubrey Hall for help instead of Moon Hollow?" Sebastian sounded sincerely curious.

"He was headed toward Aubrey Hall. I thought he might have family nearby."

Sebastian glanced over his shoulder at the villagers, his eyebrows raised in question. "Is anyone missing this morning?"

The farmers shook their heads.

Sebastian shrugged. "Search the woods."

He helped, studying the ground with the practiced eye of a hunter as everyone fanned out.

The messenger boy who had run for Aubrey Hall came loping back to me, panting for breath.

"I told them at the hall," he said. "They said the master was out, but they'll send word to him."

I raised an eyebrow and glanced to where Sebastian had circled away.

"Oh, there he is!" the boy said cheerfully, as though it was all his doing.

"Thank you," I said.

But how had Sebastian known there was trouble if the messenger had not found him?

Sebastian made his way back to me. "Could you have dreamed this injured stableboy?" he asked loudly enough for everyone to hear.

"I'm sure I did not!"

"Perhaps you misjudged the extent of his injuries." Sebastian smiled that fox-like smile of his and looked back at the villagers. "Everyone had best get back to your fields."

They nodded and shuffled off, looking none too pleased with me. I glared at Sebastian.

"I know what I saw!"

"Perhaps you do, but without any proof, what are you going to do? It might be best if you kept your night visions to yourself, little falcon."

I stared down at the ground, refusing to meet his eyes. And I saw the blood there, spattered on some of the dry leaves littering the forest floor. Dark speckles also stained Sebastian's breeches. I did not dare look up at him. Did not dare speak for a moment. Then I met his eyes. They sparkled with grim amusement.

"What have you done?" I asked.

"I have done what is best. You would be wise to forget what you saw."

He bowed and strode away. Only then did I unclench my hands and draw a long, shaky breath. I was not an idiot, and I was not imagining things. The blood proved it. But who would believe me? I considered telling Uncle Barabbas or Aunt Berenice, but the thought of confessing my nighttime spying cut the idea off before it could take flight. They would think me meddling or wicked as the rest of my family did. And there was no way to prove that the blood was Jim's. What if they didn't believe me? Called me a fluff-brained girl? I had to unravel this problem on my own.

6

JIM'S DISAPPEARANCE LEFT ME WITH TWO POSSIBILITIES. Either Sebastian had found him before I brought help back and had, for reasons I could not guess, taken the boy, or else whomever Jim was running from had caught up with him.

I stared at the blood on the ground. Like the blood on Sebastian's breeches. At least, I thought that was what the dark stain was. I hated to think of him as the villain, though. He reminded me too much of myself: a black sheep. Did the black sheep always have to be the wicked one? Could we never find a place in the flock?

I tracked Jim's path back toward Moon Hollow. The river slithered under the glow of dawn. Why had Jim said the river hurt him? He had been running from someone. Or some*thing*. The ghost, perhaps? Had it tried to drag him under, and he escaped? He had warned me away from the water, though; I did not think him foolish enough to go for a swim in the dark.

There were plenty of other people at Moon Hollow for him to flee. My uncle had visitors and guests in and out every day. Had Jim learned something he was not supposed to know? But he had run for Aubrey Hall, not my aunt or uncle or even Moll. So, either he was fleeing someone at Moon Hollow or he was trying to reach someone at Aubrey Hall. Or both.

Sebastian seemed very interested in what happened at Moon Hollow. Had he sent the boy as a spy?

My first reaction was indignation on my family's behalf, but then the idea gave me pause. Why *was* Sebastian so interested in Moon Hollow when his real concern seemed to be some debt he owed to Aubrey Hall?

So, my circling took me back to Moon Hollow. The big house stood serene in the early morning light, its windows blank reflections of the cloudy, leaden sky. But the peace might be a lie. I walked around the house, trying to spot a crack in its facade where its secrets might spill out. This was my last chance at having a home. No scandal or tragedy could be allowed to spoil it.

The other stable hands would know more about Jim.

A group of horse-grooms employed by my uncle and his guests sat outside the stable, laughing at a joke from one of their fellows. They quieted when I approached, their expressions ranging from curious to slightly annoyed.

"Good morrow," I said. "I'm looking for the stableboy, Jim."

One of the horse-grooms who worked for my uncle raised an eyebrow. "Is he in trouble, then?"

I smiled. "Not at all. He told me he would introduce me to uncle's horses."

"I'd be happy to show you around the stables," another man said, a suggestive twinkle in his eyes.

"I'm sure you would, but I believe Jim would be a more intelligent guide."

The other grooms laughed, and the roguish one chuckled good-naturedly.

"She's got you there," Uncle's groom said, then turned back to me. "Jim is a bright fellow if a bit over-eager. I've not seen him this morning, though. He might have popped into the village to visit his old man."

"He's from the village, then?"

"Born and bred, like most of us at Moon Hollow. If I see him, should I tell him you've been by, Mistress?"

"Aye, do."

But I did not think they'd see Jim anytime soon, and Jim was from the village, not Aubrey Hall.

Master Grubb was the schoolmaster, and he knew Jim.

I wandered the estate, following the scent of chimney smoke coming from somewhere near the river. Master Grubb's leased lodge could not have been far. When I glanced back toward Moon Hollow, I thought I spotted the tall, red-headed figure of Robin the porter lurking in the trees behind me, but when I turned to see more clearly, no one was there. I frowned and pressed on.

The smoke led me to a low, boxy building hidden by the trees upstream from Moon Hollow. With the oak door looming before me, I hesitated. What would Master Grubb think of me wandering to his lodgings?

Then I remembered Jim bleeding on the ground and screwed my courage to the sticking-place.

Master Grubb answered my knock himself. A smudge of soot crossed his forehead, and I wondered if he cooked for himself, too. No wonder he ate often at Moon Hollow.

"Mistress Hawkins?" He glanced around the clearing as if expecting to find someone else.

"Master Grubb. I'm looking for Jim, the stable boy, and wondered if he was one of your students."

His forehead wrinkled. "Aye, Master Coffin asks me to teach all of his servants enough that they can read the Bible and do basic sums. Is Jim not at the stable?"

"He's not."

"That's not like him. He loves working there. I have to drag him away for lessons."

"You'll keep an eye out for him, then?"

"I will."

"Was there anyone at Moon Hollow—or in the neighborhood—who bullied him? Whom he might hide from?"

Master Grubb shifted and looked away. "I cannot say for certain that I would know..."

"He might be in danger, Master Grubb."

The schoolmaster met my eyes, his expression pained. "I'm sorry. I cannot say... I need to leave soon for the church. I have a class waiting. But I'll see if Jim is there. The little rascals usually know what's going on in the village." His voice carried a false lightness.

Was it someone at Moon Hollow that frightened him, or someone in the village? "If you teach at the church, I suppose your pupils are from all over the parish."

"I teach anyone willing to pay, and the great families of the parish sponsor students as well."

"Do you have many pupils from Aubrey Hall?"

He gave me a quick, curious glance. "Not many. They cannot afford it."

"Master Westwood is a poor manager then!"

"As to that, I cannot say. Probably. The Baroness de Aubrey assigned him care of Aubrey Hall after her guardian Lord Blacknall died. That knave left the tenants barely surviving. If

Master Westwood is anything like him, he'll drain the place dry."

"What a pity," I said, trying to reckon this view of Sebastian with what I had seen.

I wandered back to Moon Hollow, worrying over Jim. The constable visited my uncle from time to time. Maybe I should tell him the boy was missing.

A servant girl scurried up from the side of the house, clutching something in her hands. The servants kept their distance fro me, so I could only guess what secrets they might keep. The girl gave a start when she saw me, and her eyes grew wide. She looked like she would say something but ducked her head and ran for the kitchen door.

Interesting.

A well-worn path led to stairs going down. The cellar. Strange place to build it— inconvenient for the servants.

I took the first few steps hardly even thinking of it, but then I hesitated as the dank smell of the cellar billowed around me. It was dark, even in daylight. The kind of place an unhappy spirit might linger while the rest of the house bathed in sunlight.

But the servant had looked surprised to see me like I should not have been there. That was enough for me.

I rested my hand on the worn wooden door, then pushed it open and stepped inside. I left the door ajar since I had not brought a candle.

The cellar contained barrels of salted meat and root vegetables, all typical and innocent. It seemed a shallow room, but there was a faint draft moving through the space. I felt along the edges of the beams and stones until I came to a gap. I slipped my fingers into the crack and found the cold metal of a hidden latch. I lifted it. A narrow wooden door swung open, revealing a gaping cavern beneath the house. Cold, musty air rushed around me.

I stood on the threshold, waiting for the wail of a ghost, but the empty darkness waited in stifling silence. I could not see well enough to chance even a step into the dank mouth of the cavern. Instead, I pulled the door closed again and hurried up the stairs. I would have to come back with a candle.

In the daylight, I blinked and tried to make sense of what I had just seen. Secret rooms under the house. The building itself was very old. Who knew how long that cavern had been there and what it might hide? I shivered despite the sun's warmth and walked back to the gardens.

On the path before me, I caught sight of a wispy woman in a pale dress drifting toward the river. I froze. Was it Moon Hollow's ghost? Or had Faith's white lady followed me?

7

MY MOUTH WENT DRY AT THE SIGHT OF THE PALE LADY. But it was no ghost. It was Sybil. Headed right for the water.

"Sybil!" I called.

My cousin paid no heed. I raced across the garden, dodging low boxwood hedges and shrubs to reach her before the river claimed her.

"Sybil!"

Her spaniel squirmed out of her arms and raced a safe distance from the river to run in circles and bark wildly.

She took the first step into the water. It swirled hungrily around her foot.

I grabbed Sybil's arm and swung her to the riverbank. She stumbled back onto the ground, blinking up at me in confusion. Her pupils were too wide, the black swallowing most of the gray.

"Sybil, what are you doing?"

"The water is so beautiful. I wanted to feel it. Like Moll."

"Moll?" I helped Sybil to her feet and wrapped an arm around her to guide her toward the house.

"She came from the water."

"What do you mean?"

"Mistress Sybil!" Moll raced through the garden, her eyes wide with panic. She gasped when she saw us and threw her arms around Sybil. "Mistress Sybil! That was very naughty. You should not leave the house!"

Sybil looked down, pouting.

"She went to see the river," I said.

"Heaven help us!" Moll squeezed Sybil tighter. "'Tis very dangerous, dear child. Never do that again."

"But you came from the river." She pointed to the shell Moll wore on a cord.

Moll sighed and looked at me. "My father is a sea captain." She looked back at her charge. "But I did not arrive here by swimming. And I never want to see you on a boat, Mistress Sybil. You keep your feet on the land as God intended."

Sybil pouted again, but she nodded. I relinquished her to Moll's care.

"Thank you," Moll said to me, her hostility gone.

I nodded and smiled weakly. Perhaps I had the start of an ally at Moon Hollow.

Hinton pounced when I entered the house, like a frog after a juicy moth.

"The mistress wishes to see you in her drawing-room."

I nodded and headed upstairs. Aunt Berenice waited for me with a man carrying shears and a measuring rod. The tailor. Time for humiliation.

"Jael!" my aunt said. "You were abroad early."

"I was looking for the stableboy, Jim. He was going to show me the horses, but I cannot find him."

"Do you like to ride?" Berenice asked. "We can have an appropriate safeguard skirt made for you, too, to keep your dress clean."

"I'm not... an overskirt just for riding?" I had rarely even owned a new dress. "That's not necessary. But young Jim—"

"Later, dear, the tailor is waiting. We need to decide what you should have." She looked at the man. "Lace collars, of course. And two small slashes in her sleeves—modest but fashionable. What colors would look best?"

I stood, stunned into a rare silence, as the tailor rambled on about fabrics and took measurements. When he stepped away to mark on some fabric with his chalk, I sidled up to Aunt Berenice.

"You need not do this."

She glanced at my worn, made-over gown. "We want you looking your best now you're part of the family. Surely, you would like a new dress."

"I would!" I lowered my voice further. "But the cost..."

"Your father's solicitor sent your stipend. You can afford it."

I was once again at a loss. I could afford new dresses. My father had not entirely forgotten me, then, and Aunt Prudence had likely been cheating me. The tightness that always knotted my belly eased a little. I was safe with Aunt Berenice now.

The tailor cleared his throat and displayed several fabric swatches. "Blue and yellow are fashionable, and pale colors are appropriate for young ladies. On this one's figure," he motioned to me, "red would be eye-catching."

Red like a fox. Sebastian's image flitted through my mind, and I smiled. To be free from dull Puritan blacks faded to a sad gray. To be eye-catching. The idea stirred a guilty thrill, and I reached for the fabric he held out.

But Aunt said sternly, "Red is overly bold for a modest girl's dress, do you not agree?"

The tailor kept his face impassive.

I pulled away from the delightful red fabric. I knew how quickly my brash manners could scare away affection. Instead, I held out my hand over the other fabrics like a divining rod, trying to determine which choice would reward me with approval. Watching Aunt Berenice's reactions, I selected a soft blue and an aggressive shade of yellow that bordered on orange. She smiled on me with favor.

"And perhaps the red for a cloak," I said, daring to be just a little bold.

Aunt Berenice raised an eyebrow at the choice but did not object or turn a loathing gaze on me. I allowed myself a small smile. I could win this game. The rules for gaining acceptance were not so strict at Moon Hollow.

The tailor made more measurements and chalk marks as my aunt and I discussed fabrics and sleeves. I imagined for a moment that it was my mother laughing with me about over-puffed sleeves and shaking her head at a hideous ribbon. My mother would have loved me, at least, even if no one else did. I ached with a longing to remember her smiles. Had she and Aunt Berenice been close when they were children?

Too soon, the tailor was promising to have the dresses completed in a fortnight and rolling up his swatches and chalk-marked fabric.

"Hinton!" my aunt called.

The lumpy, bug-eyed man appeared in the doorway.

"Please see that this man is paid."

Hinton bowed and escorted the tailor out.

"A good morning's work!" my aunt proclaimed, fanning herself and smiling. "Sybil does not care much for fashion. She is a sweet child, but her mind is somewhat distracted. If I had another daughter..." Her fingers found the carved piece of wood hanging at her belt and brushed it wistfully. "Well, I enjoyed myself immensely today."

I returned her sad smile, my chest tight. Poor aunt! To be surrounded by guests but aching with loneliness. I would mind my naughty ways so I did not cause her more heartache.

8

I NEEDED TO DISCOVER WHAT WAS IN THAT SECRET CAVERN
—to be sure it did not relate to Jim's disappearance or threaten
my new home—and I needed to do it when no one would catch
me exploring. Nighttime belonged to ghosts and dawn belonged
to servants. That left me the evening.

Once the servants were busy in the kitchen with supper, I
took a candle from my room and snuck down to the cellar. I
listened at the door for several moments, my hand clammy on
the candlestick, leaving a brassy smell. Nothing stirred.
Quickly, before either ghosts or servants found me, I slipped
into the dim coolness of the cellar.

In the candlelight, the latch was harder to find. Instead of
relying on my eyes, I closed them and felt along the gap until
they brushed the metal latch. Once again, I swung open the
secret door. This time, the orange glow of the candle spread
before me, revealing a huge space under the house, half natural
rock and half man-built stone walls.

Wooden casks created a labyrinth before me.

My first thought was of gunpowder. I shivered. Everyone had heard of the Catholic attempt to blow up king and Parliament when James had been on the throne, but the Coffins were, if anything, of a Puritanical bent like the rest of my family. Of course, now the Puritans hated the king, too.

I backed away from the secret cavern. Perhaps I did not want the burden of knowing. Of having to decide what to do with the knowledge. I was, after all, just a foolish girl. Tired of always feeling like a burden. Moon Hollow was the closest I had come to feeling like I was wanted, or at least tolerated. The Coffins—Aunt Berenice with her motherly concern and Sybil with her childish innocence—were the closest thing I had to a real family. Maybe Moll was right, and I should not borrow trouble.

But it was too late. I knew the casks were here, sitting beneath Moon Hollow like a rotten egg under a hen. What if housebreakers or rivals had put the casks in place?

I shut the door behind me and tapped on a cask. It gave a full, dull reply. I pushed on it. Heavy. Too heavy for me to shift easily. And it sloshed a little.

Ale or wine, then? I found the stopper and unplugged it to sniff. Definitely wine. Why hide it behind a secret door? Housebreakers were unlikely to make off with anything so awkward to move.

I wandered the rest of the cavern, half expecting to find skeletons shackled to the wall or other ancient horrors. In one place, smoke stains blackened the rough wall. I examined a pit with burnt charcoal. Had someone been hiding in the cave, trying to stay warm?

A faint breeze that smelled of river reeds and fresh air wafted through the cavern. I held the candle high and noticed a deep shadow in one of the walls. A niche of some kind. But as I approached, the darkness retreated into it. A tunnel. A secret way to the river.

I turned back to look at the wine safely hidden from prying eyes.

Because it was smuggled.

Smuggling wine from France to avoid the outrageous import taxes was just another way of getting revenge on a king whose policies were unpopular. Better than gunpowder but still illegal. It was possible a stranger used Moon Hollow's cellars for smuggling, but unlikely.

I hurried back up the stairs, trying not to look over my shoulder at the smuggler's den.

The fresh air of the yard cooled my worries. Many wealthy men smuggled wine. It was an innocuous crime. Moon Hollow's neat gardens promised order and peace.

I stopped short to see a man in the doublet and breeches of the middling class pacing between the stables and the house, his expression grim. He was not trying to hide, so he was probably not a bandit, though he looked like he might do someone harm if his temper snapped.

As I stood hesitating, his gaze fell on me, and he stormed in my direction. Running would look foolish, so I held my ground. He smelled of roasting meat and fresh bread and ale.

"Begging my pardon, my lady," he said in a way that was not at all polite, "But do you happen to be a guest of the Coffins? They've always got people coming and going, it seems."

"I am their niece."

His eyes narrowed. "I imagine they have time to see you, then. I told that high-and-mighty Hinton that I needed to speak with them, but they still keep me waiting."

"My uncle is busy, but he does not mean to be rude."

E.B. WHEELER

"Does not mean to be! Aye, probably not. But if he'd only pay attention instead of frittering away his time. Look at this!"

He held out a coin.

"A sixpence," I said, not certain what I was to make of it.

"Hardly a sixpence any longer! Look how the edges have been filed and clipped. These pass through my tavern every day, and what am I to do? I hate to turn away people's hard-earned money, but I'll not be able to pay my own creditors with coin like this."

I examined the coin. He was right. Bits of the metal had been shaved and cut away until it was much too small and light. People sometimes trimmed a little gold, silver, or copper off the edge of their coins to make the precious metals go farther— illegal but winked at by all but the king's agents—but this one had been badly abused, the clipping cutting away at the image of King Charles. This was treason. A man could be drawn and quartered for it. A woman could be burned at the stake.

"A serious problem," I said, "but what can my uncle do?"

"Tell the constable to leave me be, for one thing. He thinks because I've got the coins, I must have clipped them. He needs to look elsewhere, and that's a fact."

"I will mention it to them."

"Much obliged." He said gruffly. "And perhaps you could tell me where I might find my boy, Jim."

"Jim? You are his father?"

"That's what his mother tells me."

"But I had thought..." I bit my lip. Surely his father had a right to know he was missing, though he might think I was mad if I told him the details. "The stable hands believed he left to visit you."

"He's not here, then?" the tavern keeper looked alarmed.

52

"I'm afraid not. I think... he may have gone in the direction of Aubrey Hall."

"Ah, Jim, my boy! What have you gotten yourself into!" The tavern keeper implored the sky then shook his head and walked away.

I held up the sixpence that the tavern keeper had left for my uncle and ran my finger along the clipped edge. Smuggling wine would hardly raise an eyebrow in most circles, but clipping coins was dangerous. Dangerous enough that a boy like Jim might be beaten into silence if he stumbled upon the person doing it. Someone at Moon Hollow? I shivered and hurried back inside.

✾ 9 ✾

AT SUPPER, THE HOUSEHOLD ENJOYED A RARE MEAL ALONE. Even Master Grubb was missing. It seemed oddly quiet, with only a few whispered words between Sybil and Moll.

I showed my uncle the clipped sixpence.

"Bad business, coin clipping." He held it up to the candle-light. "This one's not worth much anymore. Someone got too greedy."

"Is there anything you ought to do about it?" I asked.

"Hmm. Right you are. Hinton!"

"Aye, my lord?"

"Check the coins in the money chest. Make sure we're not taking bad shillings."

Hinton bowed and left. I stared at my uncle for a moment, waiting.

"What about the rest of the village?" I prompted.

"Constable Ives will see to it. He's a decent man. And Hinton will continue paying our laborers in good coin to keep it circulating. Not my job to hunt down coin clippers." My uncle caught my troubled expression. "There, there. You're a good girl to be worrying about such things, but 'tis none of our concern."

"Of course not, Uncle." I forced a smile. I was not a good girl, but I liked that he thought I was.

"How do you like this venison?" He stabbed a piece of meat. "One of my hunters brought it down. 'Tis true what they say. The hunting is best when the moon is full."

"Aye, dear, very melting," his wife said.

I tried to detect any difference from other venison. Perhaps I did not have a refined enough palate to notice. Uncle extolled the benefits of hunting under the full moon while Moll and my aunt listened and Sybil picked at her food.

When Uncle Barabbas ran out of breath, I said, "I had an encounter with one of our neighbors. He seemed most unpleasant."

"You must mean Sebastian Westwood!" Uncle jabbed another piece of venison and dragged it onto his plate. "That weaselly meddler! What was he doing at Moon Hollow?"

I had taken the steps boldly into this conversation, but I had to tread carefully now. "I was at fault. I did not know the boundaries of the property, and I wandered into his."

"You have to be careful, my dear," Aunt Berenice said. "The woods are no safe place, especially with your uncle's hunters about."

I had not thought of that. Could it have to do with Jim? "I have seen that. I thought... I thought I saw someone injured in the woods—the stableboy Jim—but when I looked again, he was gone."

"Do you see things that no one else sees, cousin?" Sybil's voice broke into the conversation, and everyone turned to her in surprise. She petted her little spaniel, her expression dreamy as she studied me. Her question could have sounded mocking from someone else, but she only seemed curious.

"No doubt you were confused, Jael," Uncle said. "I'll ask Master Grubb to check in on the boy, though, if you're concerned. Grubb's a fine young man. Happy to have him for a neighbor and a tenant." His face brightened. "Now, there's the husband for you!"

I stared at him. I had stumbled into more danger than I realized. "Oh, well, sir, he seems congenial enough."

"He might be a little low for her, my love," Aunt Berenice said.

"Oh, his background is good enough. I looked into it before I leased him the lodge. His parentage and income are respectable. A connection I would not mind. And you're not destitute, are you, Jael?"

"I don't think I am. Mother left me something, I think, but I doubt Father would offer much. He has other offspring to worry about now."

"Shabby business," Uncle Barabbas said. "But he'll add something extra, I'll wager, just to know that he does not have to support you in the future."

"Aye, sir." He would pay to be rid of the burden of worrying about me. I was likely destined for someone like Master Grubb. He might think me a bit of an outrageous girl, but he did not act like I was a burden.

My uncle seemed to read my thoughts on my face. He leaned forward, "I'll try to arrange for you to see young Grubb more often. Then you can decide. And I'll wager I'll find you a husband by the year's end after all!"

I bit my tongue and went back to my supper. Sybil gave me a sympathetic look, and I met her eyes with a weak smile. It was the most speaking exchange we had ever had, without a word being uttered.

Later that night, a light tapping sounded at my door.

I opened it to find Sybil standing in the corridor, shifting from foot to foot.

"Quick, come." She beckoned.

Too curious to resist, I followed, automatically copying her light, nervous footfalls.

"Quickly, quickly," she said, taking my hand to guide me down the stairs.

Hinton strode down the corridor, but Sybil ducked into an alcove, pulling me with her. Hinton's lumpy figure passed without seeing us.

"He is my least favorite relative," Sybil whispered.

"He's a relative, too?" I asked, my skin crawling at the idea.

"Some distant cousin. Mother said we had to make a place for him."

I felt a moment of sympathy for the man. He was a castoff like me. No wonder he was so protective of Moon Hollow if it was the only place that would have him.

Sybil pulled me onward. I bit back the urge to laugh nervously and followed her in silence through the dim light of candles and fading sunset.

We went out through the back door and across the cool lawn. Sybil looked around to be sure we were not followed. I had a moment's fear that she was taking me into the river, but we walked to a rise above the water. Also, I calculated, above the secret tunnel.

Sybil released my hand and smiled.

"We are here!"

"Are we?" I asked.

"Father is wrong," she said, her forehead wrinkled at the

seriousness of her proclamation. "It is not because of the hunts that they called it Moon Hollow. I will show you the truth. Just watch."

Obediently, I turned with her to gaze at the eastern horizon. And as the sun set behind us, the moon's glow bloomed over the rim of trees across the river.

"Watch!" Sybil squeezed my hand.

I obeyed. The edge of the full moon peeked over the trees, the light brighter than any candle. As we stood in hushed silence, the celestial orb rose in front of us, larger than I had ever seen it and framed by the hills. A prickle of awe tingled over my skin. No wonder the ancients believed a goddess rode the moon as a chariot.

Only once the moon had made its ascent fully above the horizon did I dare to speak.

"It is beautiful. Thank you for showing me."

"I thought you would like it, too." She gazed at the moon, her gray eyes worshipful. "I love the moon, but I should not."

"Why is that?"

She looked at me fully and said in a level voice, "Because I am mad."

"You don't seem mad." Odd and childish, but not insane.

She cocked her head. "I only know what it feels like to be mad, so I cannot compare it to being not-mad. But everyone says that I am, so I must be." She glanced at my troubled expression. "Oh, don't be sad for me. 'Tis not so terrible. I have Moll. And Tattler."

"Tattler?"

"My spaniel. But, quick, we must return before Moll realizes I'm missing. She worries."

Sybil took my hand again, and we ran across the dark,

velvety turf in the bright light of the full moon. When we reached the house, she let go.

"I will go first, then you follow," she whispered. "That way, no one will know. No one will get angry."

"Thank you for showing me, Sybil."

She glanced down shyly. "I like you. You seemed like you would listen and... and understand. Because you have seen the ghosts, too. The moonlight brings them out. At least I think so. No one else sees them but you and I." She paused. "Master Grubb says he does, but I think he's lying. I *don't* like him. Goodnight, cousin Jael!"

And with that, she slipped into the house and vanished into the shadows. I hesitated to follow her, still digesting her anxious words. Behind me, the river rolled under the moonlight like a ribbon of silk. Deceptively smooth when beneath it was swift and deadly. No ghosts roamed the shore tonight. No poachers or housebreakers, either. What did it mean that only Sybil and I saw the figures in the moonlight? Was I mad, too? How would I know? Perhaps I had imagined Jim's injury.

But then I remembered the blood on Sebastian's breeches. I might be a wicked, troublesome girl, but I was not insane. Sebastian knew it was true, but Jim was the key to proving it.

❧ 10 ❧

CHURCH WOULD BE MY BATTLEFIELD. I COULD NOT GO TO the tavern seeking information about Jim, and I dared not sneak over to Aubrey Hall, but everyone would be at the Sunday services, and someone there knew about coin clipping, house-breaking, and missing stableboys.

I arrived on foot with my uncle, aunt, and cousin. Arched windows pierced the squat gray building. Once, they might have held colored glass with pictures of the prophets or apostles, but the Reformation had left them with only plain glass, letting in a light too harsh and bright for the cool stone interior. The servants stood in the back of the nave, while we sat in the front with the other gentry on oak pews worn smooth by the backsides of generations of worshippers.

Sebastian Westwood gave me his fox-like grin from a nearby pew. I stared a moment too long before pretending to ignore him.

What I planned to do was probably a sin, but based on the long list of shortcoming the rector named—many of which I could claim for my own—I did not think it would be the thing that barred the gates of heaven to me.

Envy. Wrath. Pride. Seeking out trouble.

After the long service finally came to an end, the parish buzzed with excitement for the upcoming celebration of Ascension Day. The priest and the leading men were to beat the bounds of the parish, walking the ancient boundaries and asking God's blessing on all of them for the year. But I did not feel like part of the parish, especially when I was planning to stir up confrontation, so maybe the blessing would do me no good.

And I could not help noticing that Sebastian stood outside the circles, watching. As I was.

He met my eyes and nodded with a faint smile, his eyes twinkling as though we shared a secret and everyone else was on the outside of it. But he was keeping the secret I needed to know if I was going to make my new home secure.

I walked up to him, so close I could smell the leather of his doublet. My heartbeat picked up, making me too bold.

"Where is Jim?" I asked quietly.

His smile faded a little. "Pretty falcon, I wish you could learn to trust me."

"Why would I? You—you would keep me hooded and locked in the mews."

"You want to fly free. Moon Hollow is your cage, but perhaps I can break it."

"I will not let you break anything," I said in a whisper. Then, louder, "Were you able to remove the blood?"

Several people turned to look at us.

Sebastian raised both eyebrows. "Blood?"

"The stableboy's blood. Were you able to remove it from your clothing?"

Now, most of the parish was listening with expressions

ranging from bemusement to interest. But guilt? I could not detect it. Certainly not in Sebastian. He smiled again, cold and predatory, and leaned in.

"Does Jael the tyrant slayer strike, then?" he asked, his words a low rumble meant only for me. He straightened and raised his voice for the congregation to hear. "Poor wench. Weak minds do run in families."

Someone hissed. A few people chuckled uneasily. I smiled, not letting myself shrink from the fear that he might be right. "In yours, do you mean? You may have forgotten the missing boy, but I'll wager some physician or serving lass remembers his injuries, and they will not want his blood staining them as it does you."

With that, I turned away. The whispers began, fast and sharp. Some, no doubt, were aimed at me. More would be directed at Sebastian. But with everyone talking, someone would want to tell what they knew. Secrets, like poorly buried corpses, did not stay underground for long.

Jim's father, Parker the tavern keeper, walked up to Sebastian. The crowd grew quiet. But instead of shouting at Sebastian, Parker whispered with him. He looked serious, perhaps even a little angry, but he did not rage. As if the two were in confidence. Or, they were hiding something together.

I glanced around the villagers, who had returned to their own whispered speculations, and caught the constable watching me. He sidled over and spoke to Uncle Barabbas. My uncle beckoned me. My stomach felt heavy as I marched over to face the penalty for my boldness.

"That display was hardly fitting for you, Jael," my uncle said.

"I am sorry, Uncle." Sorry, at least, that I could not have

prodded Sebastian when my family was not present to witness it.

"I do not care for Master Westwood either, but we must leave it to men like Ives here to deal with him."

"I understand, sir."

But I did not understand. At least, I did not understand why he did not berate me for making a display of our family. Hinton, standing behind my uncle, fixed me with a glare that warned me not everyone at Moon Hollow was so tolerant, yet my uncle seemed no more than mildly bemused at my behavior.

Uncle Barabbas patted me on the shoulder. "No opportunity to speak with Master Grubb today?"

I glanced around, but the schoolmaster was gone. "I suppose not."

"I think I will hold a masque," my uncle declared. "You need a husband, and it will give you a chance to know Master Grubb and the other young men of the village better. Don't you think, Ives?" he asked the constable.

"A masque would be a fine thing," Constable Ives agreed, though his eyes looked troubled at the idea.

"I'll hire musicians and dancers. If we're going to have enough to drink, I'll have to talk to my friends down the river and ask for something French."

I gave a start and glanced at the constable, but he still wore that tight, polite smile. Uncle's smuggling was no secret, then, at least not locally. Not something worth harming Jim over. But the boy had mired himself in some kind of trouble, and I was wading blindly in after him.

I WOKE ONCE AGAIN that night to a wail echoing down the corridor. I pulled the pillow over my head. Why could ghosts not haunt us in the daytime and let us sleep at night? Everyone pretended not to hear, but I was not hiding from secrets any longer.

I threw off my bed covers and grabbed a dressing gown. I peeked out the window, but the garden and river were still.

Another wail glided down the corridor. I opened the door, ready to tell the ghost to take its torment elsewhere. My end of the house was dark and the stark halls reflected the cold light of the moon shining through the windows. Voices came from the gallery at the top of the stairs, and I slowed my steps and blew out my candle when I saw light ahead.

A figure stood elevated above the people looking on. Not an airy spirit, but Sybil, balancing on the railing of the banister, a dizzying height above the hard floor far below. My stomach turned, and I pressed against the wall.

"Sybil, come down!" Aunt Berenice called.

"Shush! Don't frighten her." Moll edged forward, holding out her hand.

Sybil threw her head back, and I lurched forward, certain she was going to fall. She howled out her mournful wail.

"Be quiet!" Sybil shrieked. "Why will they not let me go? I see them, and I wish they would leave me in peace." She wobbled, and I drew a sharp breath. "I do not wish to be mad."

"Come back down to us," Moll said. "I will protect you from them."

Sybil looked across the gallery, and I imagined she saw me. Saw right into me. The others glanced in my direction, but I shrank into the gloom, and they seemed not to notice.

My cousin smiled, suddenly too serene. "Very well, I will come down."

A hoarse cry caught in my throat, drowned by the shout of fear from my aunt, but Sybil only jumped back onto the floor of the gallery in front of them.

Moll wrapped her in her arms.

Uncle Barabbas stormed out of his parlor below, still fully dressed. He looked up at the scene at the top of the stairs.

"What happened?" he asked his wife.

"Sybil was having a nightmare," my aunt said.

"Confound it, woman! I told you to keep that girl under control. What would people say if they knew?"

I retreated farther into the shadows, and I felt the searching eyes of the family sweep my wing of the house again.

"Back to bed, all of you," my uncle said. "And no more disturbances!"

I crept back down the corridor, feeling my way in the darkness. I could still see Sybil's wide, oddly serene eyes staring at me, though I should have been too well hidden in the shadows to spot. Tremors moved through my hands. Moon Hollow—my home—was a madhouse. How fitting.

Footsteps echoed behind me. Before I could turn, a hand clamped over my mouth, holding me roughly to someone's chest, and the cold edge of a blade pressed into my throat. I froze, my heartbeat pounding in my ear.

"You should be in your chamber," a raspy voice hissed in my ear. Male, probably, but disguised so I could not be sure.

"I'm sorry," I mumbled into the person's hand.

The knife bit harder, and I felt dizzy.

"Stay where you belong," the voice said. "Be a good girl. Do not seek out Moon Hollow's secrets."

The knife eased from my skin, and I nodded once. The hand slipped away from my mouth, but I did not move. I listened, trembling, to the rustle of fabric retreating and then to the silence of the corridor. I should have heeded Moll's warning. Secrets came with a heavy cost. I touched my throat, and my fingers came away sticky with a thin line of blood. Once I felt sure my knees would obey me, I raced for my chamber and bolted the door.

❧ 11 ❧

I IMAGINED THE COLD TOUCH OF STEEL AT MY NECK ALL the next week, and I watched everyone at Moon Hollow with suspicion. Was one of the servants bold enough to threaten me? The porter Robin's face had developed a nervous twitch, and Hinton always watched with his bulging eyes. Or a guest? Master Grubb spent a great deal of time around Moon Hollow, and Constable Ives came and went as he pleased.

Did my uncle and aunt wish me silenced, too?

At least the nights were quiet now. I lay awake and listened for footsteps in the corridor. Imagined a shade with a knife creeping closer. But nothing moved outside the window. The moon waned, hiding more of her face from me each night.

The following Sunday, I spoke to no one at church, avoiding Sebastian's challenging glances.

On Thursday, I dressed my hair for Ascension Day and the beating of the bounds. At least for one day, I would not be trapped in the house with someone who wished me harm.

Uncle Barabbas rode out early. He would join the other

leading men in walking the boundaries of the parish, enforcing and delineating the order of the community. We women and the servants headed out later to the town square. Though I still looked over my shoulder every few minutes, the servants were in a talkative mood, and even Sybil was smiling. Only Moll looked somber. Perhaps, like me, she felt outside of the festivities.

Aunt Berenice led Sybil and me to stand with some other well-to-do women while their husbands were out on the procession. In the village square, a group of milkmaids and apprentices raised a Maypole festooned with ribbons.

I watched their laughing figures with envy, but I would not be allowed to join in that dance, reserved for the working men and women to celebrate their holiday. Still, there was ale and music, and I could watch the tug-of-war between the men and women and cheer for the women to win.

All of the Moon Hollow servants were there. Moll stayed with Sybil. Hinton watched the other servants with a disapproving frown. The only person missing was lanky Robin, whose height and red hair would have stood out among the others.

I eased away from Aunt Berenice and scanned the crowd, wishing I could read the secrets hiding behind their smiles. Who among them could be burgling houses? Clipping coins? My gaze fell on the blacksmith.

"Are you planning on causing trouble for Goodman Brice next?" Sebastian's whisper warmed my ear.

I jumped. "Why are you not out with the other men?"

"I was not invited. I am an outsider, you see. But you did not answer my question."

"You were speaking of the blacksmith? I am only interested in him."

He leaned closer, his sharp eyes pinning me in place. "You should not be."

My breath felt tight. "And why is that?"

"I do not think he is the right company for you."

"Oh? I was just thinking that he might be troublesome."

He smiled, his gaze caressing my face. "And that intrigues you?"

I stepped back, my cheeks warm. "I am curious. Are blacksmiths often trouble? I suppose it would be easy for them to be involved in melting coin clippings."

I tried to sound innocent, but Sebastian's lips curled into that self-satisfied smirk that made his fox eyes glimmer.

"A blacksmith would have an easy time making the molds to forge coins, but he may as well make his noose while he was at it. Smiths are always the first to come under suspicion in such cases."

"You do not think he's clipping coins, then?"

"I do not think he's a fool. But why are you so curious?"

"It is one of my flaws."

"Is it a flaw? I do not think you have many."

I scoffed. "I do not know why you flatter me. I'm well aware that I am a troublesome girl."

"Who told you that?"

"My family."

"If they thought you were troublesome, they would not have invited you to Moon Hollow."

"Oh, they did not invite me. I was sent here."

His eyebrow drew together. "But why?"

"Aunt Berenice thinks she must find me a husband."

"Here?" He glanced around the little village square. "Was there no better hunting... Where was it you lived before?"

"Oh, all over. After Father decided to get rid of me—"

"To get rid of you?" Sebastian's expression darkened.

"After he remarried." I tried not to let the sting show. "First, they sent me to live with a spinster cousin some number of times removed from me. She had been fond of my mother, apparently, but she was quite old and found me too excitable. I stayed with a few different cousins for short times. Then, I went to live with Uncle Eyebrows—"

"Er, I understood that your family preferred some unusual names, but Eyebrows?"

"Oh, his actual name was John! But he had the most terrifying eyebrows I've ever seen! And I was only a child."

"But surely you did not call him Eyebrows?"

"It slipped out once or twice. He sent me away not long after."

Sebastian tried to look sympathetic, but his lips twitched. I burst out laughing at his expression, and he chuckled, too.

"You see," I said, "I am quite wicked. Words leap to my mouth without my thinking about them at all, and it always gets me into trouble."

"I'm not sure that's truly wicked. It might even be brave." He looked away. "Better than being a coward."

"You are not a coward, though. You don't have the... the posture for it."

He laughed again, but it was not a merry sound. "I appreciate that evaluation of my bearing, but I have it on good authority that I am both selfish and cowardly."

"Selfish, perhaps. A rogue for certain. But I will never believe you are a coward."

"At least, I am not afraid to dance." His eyes glittered, and he held out a hand.

I glanced at the villagers. The musicians played, and a few other young couples danced in the square. It might displease

Aunt Berenice, but before I could think, I took his hand. He swung me into the dance. I was lightheaded as if I had too much to drink, and I leaned into Sebastian's arms.

"I still need to free the pretty falcon from her cage," he murmured.

"Oh, you must not!" I said. "You have heard how many homes I have lost. I cannot lose another."

"They've been clipping wings, have they?"

I flushed. "You should not speak so. They are not so bad, though they should have invited you to the beating of the bounds, too."

"I would rather be here."

I liked where I was, too. With the music playing. With strong, sure arms guiding me in dizzy circles. With an intriguing man looking at me as though I were a fascinating puzzle instead of a problem.

"Robbery!" One of the churchwardens rushed into the heart of the village.

The music stopped. Sebastian pulled me close, his hand reassuring on my back.

Constable Ives stepped forward. "What's this about a robbery?"

"As we were beating the bounds, we came across Goodman Bates' house with the windows broken in. Bates had been beaten and robbed of his silver plate and knives."

The villagers broke out in whispers.

"This banditry is out of control."

"'Tis a bad omen."

"It all started under Blacknall."

With that, many of the villagers turned their eyes to Sebastian. The intense expression on his face was gone, replaced with his disinterested smirk.

"And it will end with me," he said. "Blacknall let this town fall into disorder and banditry, but I will see peace restored."

"You might just as well be profiting from it," the constable said.

Sebastian fixed him with a cold look. "Someone is, and nothing is going to change until you root out the cankers festering in your village." His attention snapped to the church-warden. "Go, continue to beat the bounds of the parish. We need all the order—human or divine—it can give us. I will go with the constable to investigate this crime." He scanned the crowd and motioned to the tavern keeper, Jim's father. "Goodman Parker will be our second witness."

The constable looked unhappy about this, but he did not protest. Sebastian pulled away from me, and I almost reached out for him to stay. But then he was gone. The music did not resume, though. The villagers gathered in tight knots to gossip over the latest burglary, and I was left standing chilled and alone.

🌿 12 🌿

THAT NIGHT WAS FULLY DARK, BUT IT WAS NOT STILL. Voices echoed in the corridor. I pulled my blankets closer, grateful I had bolted my door. I could almost hear what they said, but not quite.

The voice with the knife had warned me to let the secrets rest. But Sebastian Westwood thought I was brave. If I just listened at the door, my unknown assailant would not know.

I crept across the rush mat covering the floor to press my ear against the wood. But what I heard was not voices. It was padded footfalls and the clink of silver being carried.

The housebreakers!

I leaned my forehead against the door. Meddling was dangerous. The burglars were not afraid to hurt people. But I could not let them rob Moon Hollow or injure anyone in my family. I could be as brave as Sebastian thought me.

I opened the door slowly. Cool air from the corridor flowed around me. The sounds came from the other wing of the house where the family slept. I took a pewter candlestick as a weapon and crept through the dimness.

Vague figures stood whispering in the corridor. I hugged the wall, clinging to the shadows. When I reached the gallery, the voices stopped. One figure hurried down the stairs. It looked like a woman. The other figure glanced in my direction then stepped into the shadows and vanished.

I inhaled sharply and watched, my pulse pounding in my ears as I waited to see the figure reappear. The empty corridor mocked me. I tiptoed forward, holding the candlestick ready. No one stirred.

Whoever wandered Moon Hollow at night, they were gone.

Not without a trace, though. My foot bumped something on the stone floor, and it clattered, raucous in the quiet. I fumbled in the darkness and lifted a dinner knife from the floor. The metal was cold in my hand. I fled back to my chamber to bolt myself in and light a candle.

The knife's silver gleamed in the light. But this was not Moon Hollow's silver. It was too simple. I could not know for sure, but it might belong to a Goodman Bates.

My uncle would not rob his neighbors, but someone was moving more than smuggled wine through Moon Hollow. Someone who hid in the tunnels beneath the house. Someone who had beaten Jim to keep the secret and threatened me. Was it Robin I had seen? He was missing from the festivities when the robbery happened. This could not be my home as long as someone tainted the corridors with their schemes.

Constable Ives came the next morning after dinner to talk to Uncle Barabbas. He whispered something in uncle's ear, and uncle led the constable downstairs to one of the private parlours.

I made certain no one was watching and followed, holding onto the bannister as I tiptoed down the stairs, the polished wood sliding under my fingers like silk. I moved close enough to the parlor that I could hear whispered words drifting from under the door like a cold draft.

"...suspect Westwood..."

"...out of hand..."

"...stopped..."

I leaned closer. Did they believe Sebastian was the thief? He had been dancing with me, but he could have planned it. Why, though? Because the notorious Lord Blacknall had left Aubrey Hall impoverished and Sebastian wanted to restore it, perhaps. How did Jim fit in?

Footsteps marched down the corridor. I could not be caught listening at the door. I pulled at my necklace until it popped and the fake pearls rolled across the floor. I knelt to gather them.

As I picked up the last false pearl, Hinton appeared before me, his bulging eyes bright with anger.

"What are you doing down here?" he demanded.

I showed him the beads. "My necklace broke. I did not want to lose any."

He looked at them with disdain. What kind of person valued false pearls? "Master Coffin does not like to be disturbed in his private chamber."

"I was not planning to disturb my uncle. Were you?"

His eyes bugged even more, and I swept past him. I closed my fingers on the pearls, rolling them against my palm. I needed to know what my uncle and the constable said about Sebastian, but I had no other necklaces to sacrifice to the cause.

I asked Moll for a bit of linen thread and spent the rest of the afternoon trying to string the false pearls back together. The thread frayed when I attempted to press it into the narrow holes, and my needle was too wide to pass through. I put the beads aside and stared out my window at the fast-flowing waters.

It was no good. I was stumbling in the dark without a candle. I would have to risk the wrath of the unknown assailant and his sharp knife.

I ate my supper and went to bed after like an obedient girl, biding my time. Moon Hollow grew quiet, the stars providing the only light through my window. I stared into the darkness, trying to make out the river, but there were no answers there.

The corridor remained silent. I opened my door and peered out. Empty. But a pale light glowed far ahead of me. I hurried after it.

The light floated smoothly on, beyond my reach. I saw no one, the haze of the glow blinding me to anything else in the corridor. I could not guess if I was following a spirit or a creature of living flesh.

The light vanished.

I stumbled to a stop, blinking at the sudden darkness. There had been someone—or something—in the corridor. Where had they gone? Or, was Moon Hollow making me mad along with cousin Sybil?

With a huff of frustration, I turned back to my room. The tapestry on the wall caught my eye. I dimly made out the image of a fox fleeing the hunters. I touched the woven image, and it undulated like a bed curtain. Like there was nothing behind it.

The wool of the tapestry hung heavy against the wall. I grabbed the edge and hefted it, revealing a black chasm in the wall.

I rushed to my room for a candle and returned. My hand

trembled as I pulled the tapestry aside again. I half expected the chasm to be gone, a waking dream.

Cold, stale air rolled out from behind the heavy fabric. I carefully lifted my candle and found that the crack went deeper into the wall. It was lined with stones - not a fissure, but a hidden passageway. Multiple sets of footsteps swept a trail through years of dust on the floor.

I walked farther in. Narrow slits in the wall opened on the great hall below. Arrow slots! Some past Coffins must have used this to dispatch enemies invading their home. A chill draft breathed over me. Or unwelcome guests. And now, someone used it to spy on the household or for secret meetings.

I would use it as well.

THE NEXT MORNING, I watched the servants and guests at prayer and breakfast time, checking the hems of their skirts and cloaks for cobwebs and dust, but no one was so obviously guilty.

Getting caught in the hidden corridor by thieves or conspirators was unthinkable, but I had to risk it. When no one was looking, I snuck behind the tapestry. Shafts of light from the arrow holes pierced the gloom. The hidden passage did not lead anywhere. Spying seemed to be its most natural function. I could see down into the great hall on one side and a parlour and the corridor on the other.

Over the next several days, I came to know the rhythms of Moon Hollow.

The great hall brought a parade of visitors to my aunt and uncle. Leading men of the village came to gossip with them, and travelers passing through stopped to bring them news or to partake of refreshments. Even if I kept a tally, I could not make sense of who might be friend or foe.

The back corridor offered another theater for the dramas of the servants. The upper maids bickered over precedence and pecked at the lower maids to get their work done like cranky old hens. The younger girls stopped to gossip over piles of laundry. When a scullery maid and the washerwoman collided, their hidden stage flooded with dirty laundry, dirty dishes, a crying maid, several shouting women, and Sybil's spaniel Tattler alternating between licking the fallen plates and barking at the noise all with tail a-wagging.

During a lull in the daily show, I discovered a different kind of drama playing out. Robin walked along, his long legs eating up the distance, and Moll came from the opposite direction. She glanced behind her, then held out a hand for Robin.

He took her hand and kissed her fingers, his expression fixed wholly on her.

"I h-hate this," Robin said, his voice carrying to my hiding place. "How much longer must we s-stay?"

"I don't know," Moll said, her voice weighed down. "I cannot leave poor Sybil. She's just a child, and it is not safe here."

"N-not for you, either!" Robin drew her closer, and she leaned into his embrace. "I w-want us to go together, but at least get yourself safe. If you agree to my plan—"

"I told you I don't like it."

"Then appeal to your f-father."

Moll pulled back. "Not yet."

I looked away from their private moment. Robin wanted to leave. And I thought I'd seen a man and woman the night I found the silver knife in the corridor. They could be hoarding coin clippings and silver to make their escape.

Footsteps brought my attention back to the corridor.

Moll straightened and stepped away from Robin. Hinton bore down on them.

"What are you two doing here when there's work to be done?"

Moll walked past him without a word, but Robin stood shifting his weight like he might take a swing at Hinton. I leaned forward, not wanting to miss that if it happened.

"I've warned you about that woman," Hinton said.

Robin balled his fist, then relaxed and shook his head. "What would y-you know?"

Hinton stepped up to him. "I know trouble when I see it. I will not allow anything to disrupt Moon Hollow."

Robin pushed past him.

Hinton watched him go, then glanced up, as if he knew I was watching from the arrow slots.

I pulled back, my heart pounding. It might have been my imagination, but if Hinton used this place to spy on the household, he might be coming to trap me here and expose me to my aunt and uncle. I held my skirts so they would not rustle and hurried from the hidden chasm.

Once safely in the corridor, I brushed off my dress and hair to be sure I was not trailing any cobwebs. I walked calmly, but my mind was in turmoil. Secret alliances, suspicious stewards. Had Jim come across Robin's plans and been whipped out of Moon Hollow for it? But what did that have to do with Jim's warning about the river?

I had to use the secret corridor carefully, but I could not stay away from it over the next week. I felt both closer and further away from Moon Hollow as I watched its residents go about their lives without knowing I was there. What a lonely existence a ghost must have!

Only once did I catch Uncle Barabbas in his parlor with Constable Ives. They whispered together for a few minutes, then my uncle shook his head.

"Best to look the other way," he said.

"As I often do, my lord, but there are some things I cannot overlook."

"Don't be ridiculous, man. There's nothing like that going on here."

The constable mumbled a reply.

"Well, you're free to look, for all I care. You'll not find anything."

I began to fear Uncle might be right. I knew something suspicious was happening, but I could not find the proof.

13

THE MOON GREW ROUNDER AGAIN IN THE SKY, AND WITH its light, I felt a growing restlessness. Something swam just beneath the surface at Moon Hollow, and I could not grasp it.

One evening, as we ate supper upstairs in the gallery with the usual assortment of guests, Robin walked into the room, his face promising something unexpected. He shot a glance at Moll, who looked down quickly.

Robin drew himself up to his full height and announced, "Master Westwood, here to see Master Coffin."

Everyone went still. A pair of travelers from London clearly sensed the tension but did not understand it. Uncle Barabbas scowled, and Constable Ives picked at his white collar.

Sebastian sauntered into the room, a slight smile playing on his lips. He bowed briefly and straightened, watching the uncertain assembly with a glint of amusement. He raised one hand and rolled a silver coin over his fingers.

Uncle Barabbas dabbed his lips with a handkerchief. "Welcome, Master Westwood," he said, not quite looking at Sebastian. "Join us."

"Thank you." His smirk hardened as he pulled out a chair and lounging in it, surveying the meal with detached interest.

"What brings you here, Master Westwood?" my aunt asked, her tone crisp.

"I was looking for Constable Ives." He nodded to the man. "I thought he might be here." When the constable flushed red, Sebastian smiled placatingly. "Because you are such good friends."

"You found me," the constable said. "What is it you want?"

Sebastian held up the coin once again and flicked it to the man with his thumb. Ives missed the catch, and the coin clanked onto the table, rolling away. Its flat edge halted its hypnotic spiral and sent the coin tumbling over with a hard plink.

"As you can see, it has been clipped," Sebastian said. "Rather aggressively."

Ives frowned and lifted the coin. "Aye, it has. And where did you get it?"

"The blacksmith," Sebastian said. His eyes caught mine, just for a moment, and sparkled mischievously.

"And you think he clipped it?" Ives asked, suddenly all interest.

"I doubt it since he brought it to me to complain."

"Why to you?"

"That's what I wondered. He is not certain the constable would listen to him. Thinks you might have preconceived notions about who's guilty."

Ives slammed the coin down on the table. "Ridiculous! If you have been poisoning people's minds against me—"

"Ridiculous, as you say. *You* have been poisoning their minds by failing to catch the robbers terrorizing the neighborhood. By allowing their money to be clipped until it is worthless."

"I am doing what I can!"

Sebastian looked over the feast spread on the table. "I see. You suspect the Coffins, then, and you are here to make inquiries?"

"Of course not!"

The table grew dangerously silent. Hinton's round eyes looked near to bursting from his face, and Uncle Barabbas was a violent shade of red.

"They must do something with the clippings, mustn't they?" I asked quickly.

All eyes turned to me. I hoped I was not being troublesome as I went on.

"The metal does no one any good unless he sells it or melts it down. So, whoever is clipping the coins must also be forging or something similar?"

Ives' face relaxed a little. "Very true, mistress. We'll be looking for a criminal who has the equipment to melt the gold. Maybe someone who has been passing off false coins."

"Or someone who's smuggling it elsewhere." I should not have said it, but I could not stop my naughty tongue.

The constable shifted in his seat and kept his eyes focused on his wine glass. "Perhaps. But less likely. They could easily be caught."

"Of course," I said quickly. "How foolish of me."

Sebastian watched me with his quirky smile. He took a sip of the wine and said, "What excellent quality this is, Master Coffin. But, you always have it so. I look forward to the masque."

With that, he stood, bowed, and left. Robin scrambled to keep up and escort him out.

The meal sunk into uneasy quiet punctuated by stilted conversation. I kept my eyes on my plate and stabbed at my ham. What kind of trouble had I caused now?

As soon as the meal was over, I hurried away. At the end of the corridor, I thought I caught a glimpse of a woman all in white. I was careful not to look her way, but I did not think that would stop whatever new disaster I might have brought upon myself.

~

THE NEXT DAY, Moll found me in the parlor working on my spinning.

"Mistress Jael, please, Sybil needs your help."

There was more feeling in that statement than I was used to hearing from Moll. "Of course. What do you require?"

"'Tis her little dog, Tattler. We cannot find it, and Sybil is... distraught."

I frowned. "Surely the creature runs off from time to time?"

Moll shook her head. "It is excessively devoted to Sybil. And..." she glanced around and lowered her voice, "Sybil said it seemed agitated about something. It was barking and acting very strangely. And now it has vanished. It seems a bad sign."

"Of course, I will help with the search."

"Thank you."

The rest of the household had fanned out across the gardens and turf, calling for the little spaniel. They worked their way toward the river.

But the dog did not like the water. There were many places it could get lost or trapped within the house. I snuck down to the cellar with a candle, but the dog was not there. Nor was it behind the tapestry. I began checking rooms.

The door to my chamber was open. Strange. I thought I had shut it firmly. I pushed it open.

Sybil's spaniel lay stretched out on my floor, not moving. I stood stupidly for a moment, then shouted for help. I ran to the dog's form, but it did not stir at my touch. It still felt warm, but there were no other signs of life.

A wail of despair made me start. Sybil stumbled forward. Mud from the garden dirtied her skirt, and tears streaked her cheeks. She fell to her knees beside the still form of her little dog. She looked up, seeming to not see me, and back at the dog.

"Please, no!" she shouted. "Please, someone wake him up!"

Moll ran forward and wrapped an arm around her. "Shh, dear, he's not waking up again. Quiet, quiet. Before you make yourself ill."

At that, Sybil's sobs turned into shuddering sniffles, the tears still running unabated down her cheeks. She gave me an imploring look that shimmered with grief.

I knelt by the little animal again. I could see no injury to it. Whatever had killed it, it must have been only moments before. Yet they had been searching for the poor creature for some time.

I glanced at my aunt. "Please, get her comfortable. I will take care of the animal."

Sybil stared at me in uncomprehending sorrow, but her mother guided her away, with one last look back. Did she suspect me of harming the poor creature? My stomach knotted.

Moll stayed by my side, her features creased in a frown.

"I did not harm it," I said. "I found it like this."

Moll roused herself from her troubled thoughts and met my eyes. "I believe you. What do you think happened to it?"

I gently lifted the little body. "I'm not sure. It is strange. I would like to find out."

Moll nodded. "Do what you need to. We do not need to tell Sybil."

She left me alone. I kept my thoughts to myself, but whatever Moll guessed about my intentions, she was probably far from the truth. I carefully gathered the small body. It was still not cold nor stiff, and yet it showed no movement. I carried it to my bed-chamber and laid the body on the floor.

I did not think the dog's death was natural. Nor did I think it supernatural. Someone had done something to the creature and then left it in my room. To make me look guilty? Or, as a warning? I had been threatened before, and I had not listened. The message was clear: I either had to stay silent or stop them for good. And I was not used to being silent.

14

A FEW DAYS LATER, WITH THE MOON ONCE AGAIN NEARLY full, the time for the masque arrived. Sybil's little spaniel lay in my room, its body soft and warm but otherwise as still as death. Something dangerous was at play here. Maybe something supernatural after all.

"Perhaps the masque is not wise," I said to Uncle Barabbas before breakfast. "Sybil is still quite upset."

"Aye, poor girl. But she would not have liked it anyway."

I frowned. My uncle put a hand on my shoulder.

"If we canceled the masque now, people would start asking too many questions. We cannot have that. People must not know of Sybil's condition."

"I am not sure she is mad," I said.

Uncle Barabbas shook his head sadly. "'Tis kind of you to see the best in her, but her mind has always been weak, and of late it has been much worse than that."

My interest perked. "Of late?"

"The last year or two. As she has grown, so have her troubles."

"I'm sorry to hear it," I said.

But mingled with my sorrow was a painful curiosity.

Sybil's problems aside, I dreaded the thought of Moon Hollow being filled with strangers. Any of them could be house-breakers. Any of them could be potential murderers.

Moll helped me prepare for the masque since Sybil was still mourning in her chambers.

"You do not like this either," I said.

"I am only a guest of sorts here. 'Tis not my decision."

"How did you come to live at Moon Hollow?"

"My father is a sea captain and an acquaintance of your uncle."

"A smuggler?" I asked.

She raised an eyebrow but smiled a little. "Some untaxed wine may have made its way into his hold. When my mother died, my father could not take me to sea, so he asked Master Coffin to make a place for me. At first, I did not plan to stay. I did not wish to be in the way in someone else's home. But Sybil became like a little sister to me, and I found... other things to like at Moon Hollow. I realized I could make my way here. Lately, though..." She shrugged. "Something is wrong."

"What?"

"Something I cannot see. Only feel."

We put on our masks and walked down the corridor to the gallery where some of the guests watched the performers in the great hall below. Robin stood to the side, and Moll caught his arm.

"Are you going to dance with me tonight or run off and hide again?" she whispered, her lips curved in a teasing smile.

He flushed brilliant red. "I'll d-dance if you want me to, b-but I'm not very good."

Had Robin missed Ascension Day because he was embarrassed to dance? It was still possible he was one of the housebreakers, hoping to use the money to free Moll from whatever danger he perceived at Moon Hollow.

I left them alone and descended the stairs. Sebastian was not afraid to dance, and he had said he would be at the masque. I scanned the crowd assembled in the great hall for some sign of him. Candles twinkled all around me, and masked actors danced, performing a scene about Poseidon, judging by their costumes. But not a hint of Sebastian. Master Grubb bowed to me, Constable Ives frowned at me, and Uncle Barabbas introduced me, it seemed, to every man in the shire except the one I wanted to see.

The performance ended with an invitation for all to join the dancing. Hinton directed the extra servants hired from the village to deliver goblets of Uncle Barabbas's smuggled wine. And was that Sebastian lurking along the wall?

Master Grubb stepped in front of me before I could find out.

"Dance with me, Mistress Hawkins?" he asked.

"Certainly." This was why Uncle had planned the masque after all. Though, he was clearly having an excellent evening, talking to neighbors and accepting compliments on the entertainment.

Master Grubb took my hand for the stately pavane around the room. I glanced back once more for Sebastian then turned my attention to my partner. A faint odor of charcoal clung to his clothes, and a scabbed wound marred his knuckle.

"Are your students behaving themselves?" I asked.

He laughed. "Quite well."

"I wondered because of your hand. It appears you have been injured."

He did not meet my eyes. "Only a slight burn."

"Were you trying to cook for yourself?" I teased.

"Just a small experiment." He pinched his lips closed, as if he regretted speaking.

"Oh, how clever that sounds!" I said in my best 'simpering female' tone.

He puffed up a little. "I dabble in alchemy more than a little."

"You have turned lead into gold?"

His expression stiffened again. "There's much more to alchemy than that."

"How fascinating." And I meant it. Here was someone who could melt down metals.

He did not look inclined to tell me more, though.

We drank and danced, and a glow of euphoria came over me, more than just the warmth of the wine. Why was I so worried? Uncle Barabbas would not hold a masque for someone he planned to dismiss. Aunt Berenice enjoyed fussing over me like a second daughter. They were not so proper as the rest of my family. Moon Hollow was my home. I just had to mind my tongue, and I had nothing to fear.

"Niece!" my uncle called. "The dancing will make you thirsty. Have more wine!"

I downed a goblet and returned to the dancing, laughing at my partners' remarks no matter how dull. Such a good girl! My uncle and aunt would have no reason to call my manners slovenly or ungrateful. I spun in a circle, so light I might float away. Another partner took my hand, but I could hardly feel his touch. I drifted elsewhere. The candles danced along in their sconces. The portraits smiled at me. Laughed. Leered.

I pulled away from my latest dance partner, heedless of what he asked. The pictures on the wall glared now. They knew the truth. They knew I would bring trouble to Moon Hollow. I would burden or shame my aunt and uncle like I had all the others. They did not want me. The portraits whispered it, and the viols sang a jarring tune.

Naughty fool. Run away.

"Jael?" Aunt Berenice asked, her voice coming from far away. "You look flushed. Come rest, dear."

But the masked faces around me warped, growing and shrinking, staring eyes, pointed noses, and sharp, crooked teeth wavering like reflections in a pond. I shrank back from the ghastly sight. Hands reached for me, transforming into claws with sharp talons.

Devilry. A company of warlocks.

My mouth was too dry to shout, too dry to swallow, though my stomach heaved as if I were on a ship tossed by wild waves. The Biblical figures on the wall marched in solemn procession. At the end came Jael the king-slayer, tent stake in hand. She was not an Israelite. She would always be a wandering nomad. An outsider.

Waves of color washed over my vision. The room wobbled and bent, its walls melting like wax to flow down and capture me. Trapped. Trapped. Trapped.

I fled, clawing my mask from my face. Shrieks howled down the corridor after me. *Clumsy. Fluff-brained. Brat.* The words would catch me. Catch me and wrap me up and suffocate me. I could not breathe. The air itself had turned to wax. I clawed at my face and my throat, desperate to free myself from the waxen words flowing around me. Sticking me to the ground.

The back doors were before me. I fell against them, shoving them open, letting the cold night air harden the wax until it grew brittle and cracked when I fell to the ground and crawled free onto the grass.

Free.

The moon hovered above me, glorious, white fire alive in the sky. So bright. Brighter than even the sun shone. I reached to touch it, and my hand glowed as well. Maybe the moon would claim me and I would sail away into the night to become nothing but stardust. The cool, damp scent of the grass vanished, and I floated upward. Away, away.

"Farewell," I sighed.

"Mistress Jael?"

I twisted my head to the side. Sebastian stared at me, his face washed silver in the moonbeams and his eyes sharp spears of light.

"Master Westwood," I said, my words slow and slurred. "Do you live on the moon, too?"

"Would you like me to?"

"You know, I think I would. You might be a villain. I cannot decide. But I have decided you are not the bad kind of villain. We will be safe on the moon."

"Aye. Probably the only place we'd be safe now. Tell me, little falcon, what did they feed you tonight?"

"Bits of millet and rye." I laughed.

But he was right. I had become a bird. The feathers sprouted all over me, soft and downy.

"You had something to drink, too, I suspect. Nay, that would not explain it. For your eyes are too dilated. Did you use belladonna drops in them?"

"I never have. Would it make my eyes pretty, do you think? I wonder what it feels like to be pretty."

"Silly bird, you are beautiful."

"Am I? Do you like my feathers? I became a bird when you called me one."

"I suppose I must be careful with my words, then."

I rocked my head to the side. "They are like magic. But you are not a warlock. I left the warlocks behind. They only want me because they know I am wicked."

"Are you? How interesting. You hide it well."

"I have a naughty tongue."

"I happen to like your naughty tongue."

I giggled, but it hiccuped into a sob. "You are the only one, then. No one has ever liked me."

Tears rolled out of my eyes, so hot they burned my cheeks, but Sebastian wiped them away.

"They are fools," Sebastian said. "If I were worthy, I would show you what it is to be adored."

The tears came more freely. "Who is worthy of love? No one, no one."

Sebastian was silent next to me for a long moment. Then he said, "And if no one, then, maybe everyone."

"Mmm," I said, too tired to think anymore.

"Can you keep your eyes open a little longer?"

"I cannot." My eyelids had shut, though I could still feel the heat of the moon's silver light washing through me. And I was a beautiful falcon soaring through it. A dream I did not want to end, where someone might love me. "I don't want to sleep forever, though. Not like Sybil's little dog."

"What do you mean, my falcon?"

I had the sense of being lifted into the air and held aloft by strong, safe arms. I snuggled down into the scent of Sebastian.

"Her little dog sleeps, not awake or dead. Poor thing," I muttered.

Nothing else was clear after that. Some liquid was forced down my throat. I might have gagged on it. But then I was warm and safe again. And I had the strange sense that, though Sebastian was near me, I was not in danger. In fact, as I glided through the night with him somewhere close, I felt safer than I ever had.

❧ 15 ❧

I AWOKE THE NEXT MORNING TUCKED INTO MY BED WITH A terrible headache. What had happened at the masque? Fantasies of monsters and flying. And of Sebastian. I rubbed my aching eyes. What had he said? That he might adore me? Surely, a fever dream. I was not even certain I could trust him. But no one would love me like that. Everyone I had known had proved it by rejecting me. The best I could hope for was to be tolerated as I was at Moon Hollow.

So, I'd had a taste of Sybil's madness. How much of what I'd seen at Moon Hollow had been illusion? Ghosts, vanishing boys, shadows moving through the night. How could I trust my own eyes—my own mind—when everyone else saw something different? My skin felt clammy, and I curled up under my blankets.

I touched my throat. A thin scab still marked where the knife had sliced my skin. That was real. Jim was real, for he had a father who asked for him and who had served as a witness to a housebreaking. And Sebastian was real. He did not deny Jim's injuries to me, only asked me to forget them.

My flitting recollections of the masque were dreamlike, melting like fog when I tried to touch them. Not like my memories of the footprints by the river or Uncle Barabbas's whispered conversations with Constable Ives or the chill of the cavern under Moon Hollow. But vivid delirium did not just appear like a toothache.

I threw off my blanket. I was not mad. Something—or someone—had done this to me. Either they wanted me to appear mad or they had hoped to harm me while I was insensible.

Had Sebastian protected me?

My whole body warmed at the thought, but I put it aside. If someone had caused me to fall into delirium, then maybe Sybil was not truly mad either. The two might be connected.

I forced myself to rise and dress so I could join the family in my uncle's withdrawing chamber as though nothing had happened. It must not have worked entirely, since the whole household watched me curiously when I sat and bid them good morrow.

Constable Ives joined us as we ate a late breakfast, his face drawn in worry.

"Another housebreaking last night," he announced as he plopped down into a chair. "During the masque."

"Again!" Uncle drained his glass. "This is out of hand."

"I know it, sir."

"Who this time?"

"Aubrey Hall."

Uncle choked and sputtered out his ale, dabbing it off his beard. "Aubrey Hall! Sebastian Westwood must be gnashing his teeth!"

"Like all of Satan's demons."

"Then I suppose he's not the one behind it."

Ives sighed, looking disappointed. "His outrage appears genuine. In fact, I pity the robbers. They may have thought they were clever, but they've kicked a hornet's nest."

Uncle laughed. "Well, good! Let it be Master Westwood's problem."

Ives looked unhappy about this, but I allowed myself a smile. Sebastian might be an ally after all.

If the robbers were using Moon Hollow to smuggle stolen goods, they would appear in the next night or two. I glanced at Robin, trying to detect signs of guilt. His cheek twitched, and he caught my stare, looking away with a scowl.

Perhaps it was he, but I could not be sure. He could not be doing it alone. Moll's father was a smuggler, but I did not think Moll would approve of Robin stealing. Maybe Robin was working with someone who could melt down the stolen silver. Someone with a burn mark on his knuckle?

That evening, I pretended to retire to my chambers but instead snuck around Hinton's patrol and out to Master Grubb's lodge. The oily scent of burning charcoal drifted from his chimney. I knocked on the door.

After a long hesitation, the door opened. Master Grubb peered out. "Mistress Hawkins? Is something the matter?"

"I was to ask how the melting is coming along."

He looked past my shoulder, scanning the woods. "The melting?"

"I know. You do not have to pretend."

Master Grubb frowned and hauled me into the lodge, shutting the door behind us. I backed away, my pulse hammering in my throat. What had I been thinking? Fluff-headed girl! I might be about to learn firsthand what had happened to Jim.

"What do you think you know?" Master Grubb demanded.

I swallowed. No backing out now. "You are melting stolen metal."

He paled and rubbed his face. "Who else have you told? That meddling Sebastian Westwood?"

"No one!"

His shoulders relaxed. "You understand, we're doing it for the best of reasons?"

"Are you?"

"I was skeptical, too, when Robin came to me, but he convinced me. There's no harm in it."

"You're robbing people!"

"That was not us! Robin has only taken the thinnest shavings. Someone else is clipping more—stealing more, and because of their greed, we may all hang!" He blinked rapidly and looked around. "You should not be involved in this. You need to go."

As if I had wanted to be a hostage in the lodge. But he pushed me out and shut the door.

Robin was the coin clipper, then. But was he also the housebreaker? If so, I did not think Master Grubb knew. Robin was using the schoolteacher to help him amass enough money to flee Moon Hollow. But that meant that Robin would be moving the stolen items out of Moon Hollow, no doubt through the smuggler's tunnel. I just had to watch it and raise the hue and cry when I spotted him.

I snuck out to a hiding place in the bushes where I could see up the river. The entrance to the tunnel was well-disguised, but knowing what I was looking for, I could make out a little cove against the high riverbanks. That was where the housebreakers would appear.

The heavy stillness of the night settled around me, cold as river mist. My limbs grew stiff, but I dared not do more than shift my foot when it began to tingle and deaden from being pinched against the damp ground.

As the night wore on, the trees behind me rustled, yet the leaves hung limp and unmoving. I tensed. Someone was out there. The back of my neck itched as though I were being watched. Yet I dared not move. Someone could be sneaking up on me, knife in hand, and I would be bloodied like poor Jim. But if they had not noticed me and I looked, the movement would draw their attention.

A footstep sounded close to my right. I turned my head a fraction, and I recognized the figure.

Sebastian.

Could he be the thief, after all, robbing himself to throw off suspicion?

He crept farther along the path then hunkered down behind his own bush.

I almost laughed, spying on him spying on the river. And yet both of us seemed to be in for a disappointing night. The river flowed serenely on, undisturbed by smugglers, robbers, or other human concerns. We sat perfectly still as the moon rolled along her path overhead. I watched Sebastian, trying to remember the words he had spoken the night of the masque. What if I had not dreamed them after all?

Finally, as dawn approached, I hissed, "Master Westwood!"

He gave a start and looked around. I rose from my hiding spot. His eyes widened, and he stood, too.

"Where did you come from?" he asked.

"I've been here since sunset. I saw you hide."

"Why?"

"The same reason as you: to catch whoever is smuggling stolen goods down the river."

Sebastian took my arm in a tight grip. "Do you not realize this is dangerous?"

"Of course I realize! Why do you think I want to protect my aunt and uncle?"

There was no understanding in his eyes, only hard anger. "It is not your place! Go home. Leave the smugglers be. Leave me be!"

Sebastian stormed off. I sank back slowly and wrapped my arms around myself, hot shame burning through me. I was in the way. A foolish girl. How could I have thought Sebastian would be happy to see me? Would want me by his side? No one ever would.

As the moon sank to the west and the sky lightened, I slunk back to the house, hardly caring if anyone saw me.

Hinton bumped into me as I slipped back inside. He turned to walk alongside me.

"Where have you been?" he asked.

"Never you mind!" My eyes stung, but I would not cry.

"I will not have the reputation of Moon Hollow sullied."

I breezed past him for the stairs. When I looked back, he was speaking to my aunt. She listened with a frown and glanced in my direction, her eyes narrow.

Cold shot through me, and I rushed to my chambers. My chambers for how much longer? Surely, Aunt Berenice now saw me for the naughty, foolish girl I was. She would send me away. Banish her troubles as everyone else had.

I would never be wanted anywhere.

I curled up on my bed, my eyes aching and every part of me heavy, and the exhaustion of the long, sleepless night overtook me.

16

A YIP ROUSED ME FROM MY SLEEP. I GROANED AND OPENED my eyes. A small, wet nose poked at me.

"What?" I asked, rubbing my eyes.

Sybil's dog sat on the bed. It yipped again, tail wagging wildly.

I sat up. Scrambled back. Was it possessed?

The little spaniel opened its mouth in a doggy grin, tongue lolling out. It did not look possessed. It looked hale and hearty. And then I noticed the puddle on the floor.

I wrinkled my nose. "You're not a demon, then, just a naughty dog. What magic is this?"

I picked the dog up. Its warm body wriggled in my hands.

"What am I to do about you?"

It was afternoon. I left the dog and snuck through the corridors, avoiding the family until I came across Robin. I almost fled from his looming figure, but why bother? He was going to escape with Moll, and I was going to be sent away.

"Can you ask Moll to come to my chambers?" I asked.

He studied me suspiciously but nodded.

Moll met me a few minutes later in my withdrawing room. "You asked for me?"

"I did." I opened the door to my bed-chamber, and the spaniel scurried out, its whole body wagging in excitement at seeing Moll.

She took it, fending off its attempts to lick her face. "What is this? A replacement? It looks remarkably like Tattler."

"It *is* Tattler."

Moll nearly dropped the creature. She held it away from herself. "How is this possible?"

"I do not know. I only know that it looked dead, but it never felt cold or lifeless. And now it is awake again."

Moll regarded the spaniel skeptically.

"At least Sybil will have some comfort when we are gone," I said.

"Gone?" Moll looked up sharply.

"I believe I have offended my aunt. I expect she will send me..." Where? I had nowhere left where I was wanted. A sob threatened to break from my chest, but I swallowed it down. "She will send me away. And I know you and Robin plan to leave," I added defiantly.

She sat heavily on a low stool. "I want to go with him, but I cannot leave Sybil. I have a soft spot for children, and I cannot abandon her to her mother's neglect."

"Neglect?" Aunt Berenice had been kind to me. How could she not be the same to her own daughter?

Moll scratched Tattler's head, and the dog licked her hand. "Your aunt is particular in her ways. Wants everything just so. Sybil has always been shy and given to flights of fancy, not to

Mistress Coffin's liking. Robin and Master Grubb have been trying to find a cure for her—"

"A cure." I scrambled to rethink my conversation with Master Grubb. "Involving coin clippings?"

"I always thought you paid too much attention." Moll smiled sadly. "I told Robin taking the clippings was too risky, but Master Grubb says a distillation of the more pure elements —especially gold—could help purify Sybil as well and restore balance to her humors."

I sat across from her, my forehead wrinkled. Playing with alchemy was all well and good, but what happened when it was done incorrectly? "Do they give her this distillation to drink?"

"They've never successfully created the formula. Why?"

I studied Moll. Robin could still be a thief, but I believed Moll was sincere. "The night of the masque, something happened to me. I felt... it was more than just having too much wine. I thought I had become a bird. That I could fly to the moon."

"Sybil sometimes says she is a bird in her bad moments," Moll said, her eyes distant and thoughtful.

"But only recently, correct?"

"Aye. She was a dreamy little girl, but never so lost to reality."

"I think someone is poisoning her. Causing her to act mad."

Moll bit her lip. "I have often feared someone in this house means her harm."

"But you don't know who?"

"I have thought at times it might be Master Coffin. He does not like anything to disturb his merrymaking, and Sybil can be difficult. Easier for him to have her put aside and forgotten."

I could not picture my uncle hurting anyone, but a more

insidious face popped into my mind. "Hinton is very concerned with everything at Moon Hollow appearing proper and orderly. He probably does not care for Sybil's dreaminess."

Moll nodded. "I cannot prove either of them has harmed her, though."

"Perhaps Sybil can help us."

Moll gently lowered the spaniel to the floor. "Is there danger in involving her, do you think?"

"I think there is danger in not finding answers. But can Sybil handle our questions?"

Moll nodded. "Her mind is not firm, but that which bends easily does not break."

As Moll left to fetch Sybil, Robin peered into the room. "A messenger delivered something for you, Mistress."

"For me?"

"From a Sir Godfrey."

"Oh!"

Had something happened to Faith? I hurried to Robin, but the package he offered turned out to be rolled up linen embroidery. I unfurled it. It was my fox and grapes but finished so the fox now held the grapes in his mouth. Faith's work, by the neat look of the stitches.

And she had added a verse to the bottom:

WOE *unto them that call evil good and good evil, that put darkness for light and light for darkness, that put bitter for sweet and sweet for bitter.*

WAS IT A WARNING TO ME? I glanced up at Robin.

"There was a verbal message as well, mistress," he said. "Sir Godfrey's messenger said I was to trust it only to you." He looked a little perplexed by this.

"Well?" I asked.

"'You were right.' That's the message: 'You were right.'"

"Is there more to the message?" I asked Robin.

He shook his head, looking as baffled as I was. I read the Bible verse again: *put bitter for sweet and sweet for bitter*. The fox, I suspected, had found the grapes sweet after all.

"Thank you, Robin," I murmured.

He left, and I sat on my chair, studying the embroidered picture. Faith could not send me a message through her mother, so she did so through her betrothed. The grapes were sweet. I was right. She was happy, then, with Sir Godfrey.

I smiled, glad for my cousin, and I felt a moment of triumph over Aunt Prudence. I had been right and she wrong in her bitter prognosis. I traced the neat stitches of the grapes. What if she was wrong about more? My touch lingered on the smooth threads added by my cousin.

What if Aunt Prudence was wrong about me?

Slovenly. Mutton-brained brat. Ungrateful, fool-headed wench.

The words were so loud. They echoed through my thoughts

each day. Every time I made another mistake, they were ready to accuse me again.

You were right, Faith's voice whispered in my ear, and the reverberations of the other voices faded.

I stared at the fox and his grapes, my heart beating fast. Everywhere I went, no one had wanted me. I was too fidgety. Too flighty. Too naughty. What if, what if... I could not bring myself to think it. I longed for it with such aching in my chest. It would hurt too much to deceive myself.

But what if they were wrong about me?

In my fever dream, I had imagined Sebastian saying he could love me. Oh, if it could be possible! My heart quavered with longing.

Moll tapped on my door and swung it open. I started and folded the embroidery away, my thoughts still fluttering. Moll led Sybil into the room. The girl's eyes were red-rimmed, and her skin was ashen.

"Cousin," I called softly, motioning Sybil over.

She drifted to me, looking over her shoulder for reassurance from Moll.

I pulled her to the other chair. "I have something I must tell you."

"You are marrying Master Grubb and going away," she said sadly. "But you should not be Jael Grubb."

"I think you are right about that. But look."

I whistled, and the spaniel dashed in from my bed-chamber. As soon as it spotted Sybil, it raced to paw her dress, its whole body trembling with joy.

"Tattler!" She scooped up her dog and buried her face in his fur. Her shoulders shook with silent sobs. After a quiet minute, she turned her smiling, tear-stained face to us. "How? I saw him dead."

"You saw him drugged," I said gently. "He was not dead. He had been poisoned. And so have you."

"Poisoned." She looked to Moll. "Am I dead, too? I thought heaven would look more cheerful, but I am glad I should still be able to see the moon here. This room is like a mirror of mine. It even looks out on the river."

"Poor dear," I said. "I'm sure heaven is lovely, but none of us are dead."

"But... I was poisoned?"

"You were given something that affected your mind. I did not realize it until someone poisoned me, too. All the things you've talked about—I felt them too. Sybil, you are not mad. Someone is doing this to you."

She held her dog close. "But, everyone says I'm mad."

"Not everyone," Moll said, resting a hand on Sybil's shoulder.

I gripped Sybil's hand tightly. "The others are wrong."

"But, they say—"

"You have to learn not to believe what they say about you." As did I. "Sybil, I think you are bright and creative."

"Really?"

"I do. So, perhaps you can help me discover who did this to you."

Hope flashed in her gray eyes. "'Tis always around the full moon."

"You like to watch the moon."

"I do."

I straightened. "You see ghosts at the full moon. Down by the river?"

"Aye. With their boat."

"'Tis not a ghost. 'Tis someone who does not want to be

discovered. And someone who has access to you. That's the trick. It cannot be just anyone."

"Someone in our household, then?" She clung to Moll. "Why?"

"They have a secret you could have unwittingly revealed, but no one would listen if they thought you were mad. The question is who. Who could have access to your food?"

"Why, anyone could."

Moll nodded.

"But it would have to be something only you eat since you are the only one who gets ill." I recalled something hazy that Sebastian had said about eyes. Dreamy-looking eyes like Sybil's. "Do you use belladonna?"

"Mother would never allow such vanity. She even gives me purgatives to keep me humble and obedient."

I sat up straight and glanced at Moll, whose eyes widened.

"She gives Sybil something special to drink?" I asked.

"When she becomes agitated," Moll said.

"Do you know what it is?"

"Just some roots and herbs, I think."

"Roots." I frowned. "The thing that my aunt carries on her belt..."

Moll shrugged. "A good luck charm, I gather."

"Mandrake root," Sybil said. "For fertility. She and father have always been disappointed that I was their only child."

"Mandrake is rare," I said. "And... poisonous?"

Sybil frowned. "Mother was angry when Tattler tried to drink my medicine one night. I thought she might have been the one who hurt him," she whispered, snuggling the little dog.

I exchanged an alarmed glance with Moll. "Perhaps she was. As a warning to me. To protect the smugglers."

"Everyone knows the wine is smuggled," Moll said.

"But what if it's more than wine?" I paced to the window to stare at the brown-green river. "There are people in and out of Moon Hollow all the time. If they know about the wine, 'twould be easy to smuggle other things as well. But why would Aunt Berenice want to protect them?"

I turned back to Moll and Sybil, who both shrugged.

"Blackmail," Moll suggested. "Everyone has secrets, and the Coffins don't like people to know their business. Or they could simply want a share of the money."

I nodded. "If we are right, and the villains are using Moon Hollow as a base for smuggling clipped coins and stolen plate, they would want to melt it down to make it harder to trace. I don't think Master Grubb is helping them." I chewed my lip. "Oh, I *am* a fool!"

"What?" Moll asked.

"In the cellar, there was a place for a fire. They could be melting the coins down there. Come, we have to find out!"

I took a brace of candles. We hurried down the servants' stairs at the end of the corridor and around to the cellar. Moll checked to be sure it was clear, then we ventured into the secret room.

"Here!" I showed them where the charcoal darkened the floor and smoke had stained the walls.

We bent low to examine the ground, sifting through the remnants of the fire.

"Silver!" Moll held up a blackened bead and rubbed the soot from it. "Someone *has* been melting it here."

"And Aunt Berenice was hiding it," I said.

Moll's eyes glittered with anger in the candlelight, and Sybil sank against her.

"Then my mother was poisoning me?" Sybil looked

between us, ghastly pale in the dim light. "My own mother? Does she hate me so much?"

"Oh, poor child!" Moll wrapped her in an embrace and let her sob out her heartbreak.

"It is not a problem with you," I whispered, stroking Sybil's hair. "'Tis a problem with her." But I knew well how little comfort that would bring.

❧ 18 ❧

"I'm going to raise the hue and cry," I whispered as Moll comforted Sybil.

"Going where?" Moll asked. "Even the constable is under your uncle's thumb."

I smiled a little. "Master Westwood is not. You should not stay here."

Moll nodded.

I rushed upstairs to grab the silver knife as proof of Moon Hollow's role in the crimes then snuck back down to the garden.

Sebastian did not want to see me, but I could not afford to worry about that. My heart beat faster thinking of his fox smile and how safe I felt dancing in his arms. It should not betray me so.

The woods loomed in the gathering twilight, its branches grasping talons in the dimness. The river gurgled along, the quiet splash of oars the only hint I was not alone. But if smugglers moved on the river, thieves might move in the trees. I hoped the shadows would work on my side as I ran light-footed down the path.

Tree branches shivered in front of me. I veered to the side. A scruffy man lurched into my way. I whirled to flee, but rough hands grabbed me and covered my mouth before I could scream. Two dirty men inspected me as I glared at them.

"What have we here?"

"Just a woman."

The hand on my mouth relaxed, and I drew a breath to scream.

The second man caught my throat. "But why is this one running about at night? A very naughty wench, I'd say." He laughed coarsely.

Naughty, indeed. I slammed my boot down, scraping my heel along the first man's shin and crushing his toes. He howled in pain and loosened his grip. I yanked the silver knife from my belt and jabbed it into the other man's arm. He swore and staggered back.

I bolted into the trees, no longer concerned about staying quiet. Branches snagged my hair and dress like clawing fingers, but I snapped free and wove through the trees. Shouts echoed behind me as my pursuers stamped and smashed their way on my trail.

I broke through into a clearing. An old stone keep loomed in the moonlight. Aubrey Hall.

"Help!" I screamed at the top of my lungs.

A hand caught my wrist. I smashed my fist against it, wishing I had not left the knife behind.

"Hush, falcon."

"Sebastian!" I gasped.

The warmth in his eyes melted through me, everything else forgotten for the moment.

"My darling tyrant slayer, why can I not keep you from running headlong into danger?"

He did care about me then. It had not all been a dream. I threw my arms around him. He seemed uncertain for a moment, then gathered me in and held me against the safety of his chest. I ached with a desire to stay there forever.

"They're in the woods," I said, my voice muffled in his leather doublet. "Thieves. Smugglers."

Sebastian nodded, his face grim. He held a pistol in his free hand. "I expected them this night. Last night, too. But I do not want to be responsible for any injury to you. I could not bear it."

I pulled back. "You would not be responsible if it is my choice. Why do you think everything falls on your shoulders?"

He shrugged. "After my father left, everything did. My mother, my siblings. I tried..." He looked out into the distance. "I did what I thought I had to, but my choices only led to more disgrace. Everyone said I was a scoundrel like my father."

"They were wrong! They did not know you."

He reached out to touch my face. I leaned into his caress.

"Ah, falcon, someday, when my slate is clean—"

"Do not wait for someday," I whispered.

"The things people would say— "

"I am through listening to them." I pulled away regretfully. "But first we must stop the thieves."

"Ha! Let them come." He gestured into the darkness behind him. "I have a dozen hearty men loyal to Aubrey Hall ready to dispatch them and put the neighborhood in order again."

"But the men in the woods are not the ones... That's what I was coming to tell you. The tunnel is under Moon Hollow, and the dog is not dead!"

"You mentioned the dog before. I'm afraid I still don't understand your meaning."

I explained what we'd deduced about Aunt Berenice covering for the smugglers.

"Mandrake can be used as a poison, can it not?" I asked.

"Mandrake! Aye. Surgeons use it to induce a death-like sleep in their patients, and to calm those with troubled minds."

"Then 'tis Mistress Coffin indeed!"

"Mistress Coffin!" Sebastian said. "I had suspected Master Coffin, but I could never catch him moving the stolen goods. The common thieves are easy enough to track or chase from town, but I needed to hunt down their leader. I was beginning to fear he was a ghost."

"There is a smugglers' tunnel under Moon Hollow leading to the river, and he had my aunt's help."

"No wonder I could not pin them down." Sebastian whistled, and several more men jogged toward us. "I've been trying to catch them every full moon for months now. Apparently, I just needed a little help."

I grinned. I was not a burden. Though Aunt Berenice would certainly regret taking me in. I felt a twinge of guilt until I remembered that she was poisoning my cousin. She had poisoned me.

Jim Parker trotted up to Sebastian. "Everything's ready, sir!"

"Jim!" I said. "You are well?" Only a healing pink mark on his forehead showed how badly he had been hurt.

"Course I am, m'lady! Master Westwood patched me up just fine, and me dad said I should stay on at Aubrey Hall."

Sebastian grinned, his eyes twinkling wickedly. "Oh, aye, our friend Jim has been safe with me this last month after his run-in with the housebreakers at Moon Hollow."

"I suppose you were going to tell me eventually?" I asked, hand on my hip.

"Naturally. And I suppose 'tis no good telling you to stay behind."

"Of course not. I'll just follow on my own."

He smiled. "I would not want you any less spirited. But it will be dangerous. A woman ready to poison her own child might go to any lengths to protect her secret."

"They are my family. They must be stopped."

He motioned for his band of men and offered me his arm. We led the way through the woods, the footsteps behind us a constant rustle through dried leaves. The last of the sun's rays were only a memory, but the moon gave us her light.

When we reached the edge of the woods, Sebastian released my hand and turned to his men. "Mistress Hawkins will tell you where the exit of this secret tunnel is."

I pointed it out to them, explaining how it connected the cellar to the river. Their eyes widened when they made out its location, disguised as it was along the rise of the riverbank.

"Spread out," Sebastian whispered. "We'll rush them on every side and pin them against the river."

His men moved like shadows, melting into the heaviest darkness under the trees and along the edges of the garden.

Sebastian pulled me close. My pulse, already quick with excitement, hammered in my throat as he leaned in, his eyes on mine, his lips curled in a teasing smile.

"Let my men do the hunting tonight, falcon."

"Very well," I said breathlessly.

He smiled and stepped back but kept his hand on the small of my back. With another whistle, he signaled his men to move. I snuck into position so I could watch.

The smugglers had pulled a barge into the little cove at the mouth of the tunnel. It lay low against the dark water, barely visible. From my angle, I spotted several men loading the barge with several small trunks, heavy by the way the men strained to carry them. So distracting was their burden, that at first, they did not see the shadows converging on them.

One of the smugglers caught the movement on the cliff above him and shouted a warning.

"Don't move!" Sebastian raised his pistol.

His armed band charged the smugglers, but one of the criminals dived for the barge.

Sebastian fired his pistol. The gun coughed orange flame. Its thunderous report boomed over the still grounds of Moon Hollow.

The smuggler on the barge responded with a shot of his own. Sebastian jerked as the ball hit home.

✣ 19 ✤

SEBASTIAN DROPPED HIS PISTOL AND DOUBLED OVER. I gasped and scurried forward, heedless of the fight along the riverbank.

"Sebastian!"

He clutched his bleeding arm, his mouth curled in a snarl of pain. "I'm not dead yet, pretty falcon. But we have to hurry. That will have roused the house." He raised his voice. "To me!"

Most of his men were distracted with subduing the smugglers, but several broke away to follow. Sebastian jogged unsteadily toward the house. I lagged behind, feeling like the worst sort of traitor.

"Is Master Coffin really a criminal?" Jim asked, peeling away from the shadows to follow us.

"It seems that way," I said with a sad smile.

"Too bad. He was good with the horses. I liked him."

I winced a little at the past tense, but coin clipping, housebreaking, smuggling? Uncle Coffin would hang. "Was he not the one who beat you?"

"Never. 'Twas one of those housebreakers. I caught him skulking around near the stable and shouted for help."

He must have stumbled upon the man coming up from the cellar. I hoped Moll and Sybil had not lingered.

Once, Moon Hollow had been a fortress, but the Coffins had changed it over to be a display place. It was no defense against armed men. Sebastian and one of his henchmen broke the door open, and we poured inside.

Sebastian strode upstairs, drops of blood from his arm leaving a trail on the rush mats.

"Barabbas Coffin! Berenice Coffin!" he called. "The hue and cry has been raised against you."

My uncle and aunt rushed into the corridor, still in their dressing gowns. The servants gathered around as well. Moll and Sybil hung back, my cousin's face swollen from crying.

Uncle Barabbas stepped in front of his wife. "What is the meaning of this?"

"We have caught your people smuggling stolen property out of Moon Hollow."

"My people?" Uncle Coffin asked. "Nonsense!"

Aunt Berenice stepped back, glancing over her shoulder at the withdrawing chamber.

Sebastian strode forward. "Furthermore"—he yanked the mandrake root free from her belt—"you had your wife use this to make your daughter appear mad so no one will believe that she sees smugglers moving at night."

Uncle's mouth moved, but no sound came out.

"Mandrake root," Sebastian continued, "causes hallucinations. It can also induce a death-like state, such as her dog experienced."

Several of the maids gasped. Robin glanced at Moll, his eyes wide.

Uncle looked from his wife to his daughter, his face turning angry purple. Sybil clutched her little dog to her chest. Aunt Berenice had gone white.

"Wife?" Uncle asked, his voice raspy.

"Lies!" She glared at me.

"Check the coin chest," Moll said from behind them. "See if it is filled with clipped coins."

"Hinton has the key," Uncle Barabbas said slowly. "And Berenice has the other."

Sebastian's men closed in on her.

"I had to do something!" she screamed at Uncle Barabbas. "You were always spending, spending, spending! Where did you think the money would come from?"

"This cannot be!" my uncle shouted. "You... you poisoned our daughter? You betrayed me!"

"You betrayed us when you followed Lord Blacknall's example and neglected your duties. I had to clip the coins to make them go further. Then Hinton suggested no one would suspect if we stole a little silver."

"Hinton?" Sebastian asked, looking around the room.

"Hinton is gone!" Barabbas said.

20

"FIND HIM!" SEBASTIAN ORDERED.

"Aye, bring me Hinton!" Uncle Barabbas shouted.

The crowd dissolved into chaos. A cacophony of shouts and stampeding feet echoed down the corridor.

"Cousin Jael!"

I faced Sybil, who stood alone, pale but straight-backed.

"Moll is gone, too," she said.

"With Hinton?"

"I don't think she would," Sybil said. "She was here, then she had vanished. I did not imagine it."

"I'm sure you did not."

Robin had run off with the searchers. So had Sebastian. I gathered my skirts and hurried after them. Sybil followed, struggling to keep up. When I reached the stairs, a muffled thump made me look back.

Hinton slipped out from the secret passage behind the tapestry. He dragged Moll with him, a hand covering her mouth. She struggled but could not break his grip. He hauled her toward the other end of the corridor. The servants' stairs.

I raced down the main stairs and to the kitchens to cut them off when they reached the bottom.

Too late. The kitchen door stood open.

I ran outside. Torches lit the dusk, fanning out through the gardens and along the riverbank. Hinton would not go to the river, would he?

He had Moll. Whose father was a sea captain. A passport to escape. The riverbanks were well-guarded.

But maybe not everywhere.

I turned for the cellar door. Footsteps sounded behind me.

"Mistress Jael?" Sebastian called.

"The smuggler's cave."

He jogged to meet me and held the cellar door with his uninjured arm while I opened the latch to the secret room.

"Here!"

Sebastian hesitated. "'Tis too dark to see. I do not want you running into danger."

"I can feel my way through. There is light ahead."

A faint glow came from the tunnel. Sebastian walked up behind me, a warm presence in the chilly gloom. I took his good hand, and we made our way through the maze of casks to the opening leading to the river.

"I'll go first," Sebastian whispered, his breath warm on my ear.

"He has Moll as a hostage," I said quietly.

He nodded, and we pressed our way quietly into the gap that smelled of stone and water. The gap widened, and I glimpsed Hinton scrambling ahead of us. Toward the opening. Toward the rushing river.

Moll spotted us and shouted.

"Hinton, stop!" Sebastian called.

"Stay back!" Hinton yanked Moll closer.

She twisted, trying to free her arm. He dropped his lantern to grab her with both hands.

The barge still bobbed in the little cove. Hinton flung Moll onto it and climbed after her, grabbing the oars.

Sebastian and I ran forward. Once Hinton pushed off, the river would whisk him out of reach.

Moll shrieked. "Ghost! The ghost of Moon Hollow!"

Hinton jerked to look over his shoulder at the river. Moll smiled grimly and flung herself at the edge of the boat, overbalancing it and sending them both into the water.

Sebastian swore and kicked off his boots, splashing into the cove. Moll's head popped up from the river. Sebastian reached out, and she swam over to take his hand. They stumbled back onto the bank.

Hinton flailed and sputtered, trying to keep his head above water, but the river had him in its grasp. It swept him downstream. In the darkness, I thought I saw a pair of pale hands rise from the water to grab his shoulders. Then he vanished. The water rolled on deep and black, the moonlight glinting on the surface.

"You can swim?" Sebastian asked Moll. He clutched his arm, the deep red stain spreading down his wet sleeve.

"My father is a sea captain. He wanted me to be able to take care of myself."

"You took care of Hinton, too," he said. "We'll search along the banks, but I doubt we'll see him again."

"Fair riddance," Moll said.

I nodded. "Now, Moon Hollow can find peace."

$\sim$

SEVERAL WEEKS LATER, Sebastian, Moll, and I sat in the gallery in Moon Hollow, with Jim hovering nearby. A sling supported Sebastian's still-healing arm, and Jim was quick to bring him anything he needed.

Footsteps came up the stairs, and we all turned. Robin's tall figure appeared.

"I've c-come from Master Coffin," he said.

He plopped into a seat opposite Sebastian and I. Moll grasped his hand, and he smiled at her.

"What have the magistrates decided?" Sebastian leaned forward, good elbow resting on his knee.

"They f-felt Mistress Coffin was under strain because of the financial situation at Moon Hollow, which made her susceptible to Hinton's influence. She claimed he was behind it all."

Sebastian smirked. "And since Hinton cannot refute her story..."

Robin nodded. "We'll n-never know for certain. They'll allow her to go free, but Master Coffin is b-banishing her to the lodge."

"What about Master Grubb?" I asked.

"No one's heard a word from him." Robin's expression was perfectly innocent, but we could all guess why the schoolmaster-turned-alchemist decided to disappear after the commotion at Moon Hollow.

Moll smiled at him. "Sybil is safe, then. We can leave, if you wish."

"Or we can stay," Robin said. "M-master Coffin wishes for me to become the new steward."

Moll raised an eyebrow. "We have some things to discuss, then."

She glanced at Sebastian and me and led Robin aside.

Sebastian took my hand, sending a warm jolt through me. "I

suppose it will be awkward for you to stay at Moon Hollow?"

"No doubt."

"Then we'll have to be married soon," he said with a smile.

"Oi! Congratulations, Master Westwood!" Jim said. "She's a good one."

I flushed and looked down. "Thank you, Jim. But, I do not even know..."

"Know what?" Sebastian prompted.

"You must get permission, I suppose. I am not even certain from whom."

"I have asked your uncle as well as your father."

"My father?" My stomach lurched.

"The news surprised him. He regrets that he has not attended to you better. He will bestow a generous bridal portion, but you will probably have to arrange most of the wedding."

I rubbed my forehead. "Where to start?"

"Jim, fetch me some cider," Sebastian said, his eyes on mine and a wicked grin on his lips.

"What? Now, sir?"

"Now, lad!"

Jim ran off.

Sebastian ran his thumb down my jaw. I closed my eyes, and he pressed his lips against mine. I leaned into the kiss, warmth pouring through me.

"We start with that," he whispered.

"You are wicked!" I laughed, lightheaded. "And, you know, I am very troublesome."

Sebastian smirked. "Then I look forward to a lifetime of trouble."

I grinned and, naughty girl that I was, I pulled him in for another kiss.

AUTHOR'S NOTE

Thank you for reading Moon Hollow. If you enjoyed it, please remember to leave a review.

Studying early modern medicine gives us a lot to be grateful for in the twenty-first century. Mandrake root was used by Renaissance surgeons to induce a death-like state in their patients, though it was easy to overdose and kill the patient. Though used to treat mental conditions, mandrake root, ironically, causes symptoms such as hallucinations. Also alchemy is famous for wanting to turn base metals into gold, but it also pursued ways of purifying other elements, including those that Renaissance people believed made up humans.

Coin clipping—shaving or cutting small pieces of precious metals from the edges of coins—was a serious crime in seventeenth century England. Because it was considered treason to tamper with the economy, guilty men were punished by being hung, drawn, and quartered, and guilty women were burned at the stake.

ACKNOWLEDGMENTS

Thank you, as always, to my critique partners for their feedback on this manuscript, including the members of the Cache Valley Chapter of the League of Utah Writers and UPSSEFW. Special thanks to Rosalie Oaks for her input, and to Dan, Karen, and the rest of my family for their support.

ABOUT THE AUTHOR

E.B. Wheeler attended BYU, majoring in history with an English minor, and earned graduate degrees in history and landscape architecture from Utah State University. She's the award-winning author of twelve books, including Wishwood, The Haunting of Springett Hall, and Whitney Award finalist Born to Treason, as well as several short stories, magazine articles, and scripts for educational software programs. She was named the 2016 Writer of the Year by the League of Utah Writers. In addition to writing, she sometimes consults about historic preservation and teaches history. You can find her online at www.ebwheeler.com To find out about new releases and special deals, subscribe to her newsletter at http://eepurl.com/bqCKTr

Made in the USA
Monee, IL
05 August 2024

63347267R00079